D0550111
LOST
JOHN LOCKYER

Published by Pearson Education Limited, Edinburgh Gate, Harlow, Essex, CM20 2JE
Registered company number: 872828

www.pearsonschools.co.uk

First published by Pearson
a division of Pearson New Zealand Ltd
67 Apollo Drive, Rosedale, North Shore 0632, New Zealand
Associated companies throughout the world

Designed by Cheryl Rowe

First published 2007
This edition published 2012

19
10 9 8 7

British Library Cataloguing in Publication Data
A catalogue record for this book is available from the British Library

ISBN 978-0-43507-612-2

Printed and bound in Malaysia (CTP-VVP)

Acknowledgements
We would like to thank the children and teachers of Bangor Central Integrated Primary School, NI; Bishop Henderson C of E Primary School, Somerset; Brookside Community Primary School, Somerset; Cheddington Combined School, Buckinghamshire; Cofton Primary School, Birmingham; Dair House Independent School, Buckinghamshire; Deal Parochial School, Kent; Lawthorn Primary School, North Ayrshire; Newbold Riverside Primary School, Rugby and Windmill Primary School, Oxford for their invaluable help in the development and trialling of the Bug Club resources.

Every effort has been made to contact copyright holders of material reproduced in this book. Any omissions will be rectified in subsequent printings if notice is given to the publishers.

A division of Pearson New Zealand Ltd

CONTENTS

CHAPTER ONE

Just after lift-off, Umbro shut down the computer pilot and took the controls. Valdez watched the data screens set into the back of Umbro's seat that showed changes in speed, altitude, air pressure and direction. Twisting and turning a handheld column, Umbro controlled the ship smoothly and expertly. Neither of them spoke. Not that Valdez wanted to talk. His mind was a muddle. So much had happened in the last few days.

He glanced at an image on one of the screens. The areas of damage on Eco were worse than he had imagined. The new rainforests, which were now producing enough oxygen to support a small human population, should have been green and clouded in mist and rain, but what he saw were great strips of greenery blotched with a rusty-orange virus. Valdez shook his head. If the virus wasn't stopped, the new immigrants already on their way from Earth would be sent back and the experiment of Eco – an Earth-cloned planet – could be over.

Valdez stared at the back of Umbro's blue helmet. Sera should have been there in Umbro's place. Valdez and Sera had planned the trip together. Now he felt the familiar burning feeling in his stomach as he tried to reassure himself that his sister Sera was good and decent. She couldn't be responsible for the virus. She wouldn't waste years of work and endanger so many lives, but his thoughts always came back to one word.

Betrayal.

The word stung him. It was full of hurt and disappointment, and Valdez knew all about disappointment. For the last few years he'd been quarantined on a satellite space station. Sera had said she wouldn't grant him clearance for Eco until each new habitat – water, deserts, ice, grass and rainforests – was established. But there had been many problems for her team of biologists.

Then suddenly, just a short time ago, Sera brought him to Eco. She put him into one of the new plant laboratories to train with her most senior biologist – Umbro. Finally, Valdez was doing what he wanted most – working with his famous sister, helping to maintain the new Earth planet. That's why it was so hard to believe that she was going to destroy it all.

Betrayal.

What he'd seen. What he'd heard. What he'd not told anyone. What he knew about his sister.

Valdez took a deep breath. The shuttle pod was claustrophobic. He didn't want to be here. Why had he agreed to come on the flight when Sera pulled out? Did she want him and Umbro out of the way?

Suddenly Umbro's voice broke the silence. "It looks bad."

Valdez sighed and said, "Yes."

"I want to look at the Eastern Quarter," Umbro continued, "to see if the virus has spread there."

Valdez felt the shuttle shift to the left. Then Umbro said, "Take the controls while I eject the sample collectors."

He had flown in shuttles before, but this was his first time in a Venom. A handheld column popped up in front of him. He gripped it, a bit too tightly, and the shuttle slid to the right. A flashing red light showed they'd left their flight course.

"Easy," Umbro said.

Valdez relaxed his grip. He forgot the burning in his stomach as he twisted the column lightly and the shuttle came back on course.

"Sample collectors ejected and collected," said Umbro. "Head fifteen degrees west."

Valdez rotated a wheel bar on the column and felt a slight vibration through his fingers as numbers scrolled across a small dial, then stopped on fifteen. The shuttle immediately banked to the left and greenery, mist and low cloud filled the image screen.

"No sign of the virus in the Eastern Quarter," Umbro said, sounding surprised. "I'll take over. I want to go down for a closer look.

Valdez released the control column. He closed his eyes and the mystifying events of the last few weeks flooded his thoughts.

He had arrived on Eco just three weeks ago. His living quarters were similar to the space station –

a dome with eating, sleeping and exercise areas – but he'd spent most of his time in the laboratories with Umbro, observing trials with new varieties of plants and trees. Every now and then, Sera came in to meet with Umbro. Then, when the virus was discovered, she came in every day, sometimes staying late into the night. In the morning, Valdez would also puzzle over their scattered printouts and screwed-up sheets of scribble, trying to help solve the mystery.

The shuttle shuddered and wobbled slightly. Valdez glanced at the screens. They were flying very low, but there was still no sign of the virus.

When Sera and Umbro had realised the virus was out of control, they knew a decision had to be made about the new immigrants – either send them back to Earth or quarantine them on a space station. Umbro had wanted to turn them back straight away. Sera wasn't so sure. She said she would decide after one last observation flight. When she asked Valdez to go with her, she had seemed upset, as if troubled by something.

The shuttle was still shuddering and now made small creaking and wrenching noises, as though it was under strain. Valdez looked at the instrument console again. Everything seemed okay – no flashing warning lights or unusual read-outs.

He glanced at Umbro's helmet. He hadn't spoken since he'd taken back the controls. He must be concentrating, perhaps even unscrambling the onboard analysis of the samples that he'd just collected.

That morning, Sera had driven them both to the shuttle port by hovercart. Just before they reached a hangar, she had turned to him. "I need to talk to you. After the flight. Okay?"

Valdez had shrugged his shoulders.

The hovercart slowed outside a hangar door. "Wait here," she said. "I'll only be a moment."

She had left the cart running and disappeared behind the door.

The words came again.

Betrayal. Traitor.

What had she wanted to talk about? Did she know he had read the notes? Did she know he had overheard her?

Then Umbro had come out from behind the hangar door, got into the driver's seat and sped off, driving recklessly fast. He also looked upset and troubled. When Valdez asked where Sera was, he had said, "She's not coming. There's been a new development in the labs."

They had pulled up alongside the Venom, which was ready for launch. Umbro had stepped out of the cart and moved up the travelator. He didn't notice the compact ceramic and metal tool fall out of his pocket. Valdez grabbed it and called after him, but he didn't hear. Valdez rolled the tool in his hand. It was like an ancient penknife, but it was more than just a knife. It was a multi-function tool with a fold-out blade, a screwdriver, an awl, a pick and scissors. Although Valdez had seen Umbro use it to cut and splice plant stalks and leaves in the lab, there was no real use for it on Eco. Computers and robotics controlled everything on the new planet.

Valdez had seen Umbro standing at the top of the travelator, waving at him to hurry up, so he slid the tool into his coveralls pocket and ran for the shuttle. By the time he'd scrambled through the hatchway, Umbro was already seated and sealed in the forward pod. Then they launched and he forgot all about the tool.

The shuttle had stopped shuddering now, but it was rocking and bumping. Valdez looked more carefully at the panels and pads. Still no warning lights, but a small yellow light – the pod ejection indicator – in the corner of the main instrument console caught his eye. It was armed and ready.

"Umbro," he said into the intercom, "is there a problem with the pod ejection indicator?"

Umbro didn't answer. Valdez looked at the back of his helmet. "Umbro?"

He heard a soft moaning. Umbro's helmet twitched, then suddenly jerked backwards. Valdez felt jolts and a thump that left him breathless, almost winding him. Then a blinding light filled the shuttle pod. Valdez closed his eyes, opened them and blinked, then immediately checked the ejection indicator. It hadn't changed. Then he saw Umbro's helmet at an odd angle.

"Umbro?"

Again there was no answer.

"Umbro!" he shouted, hitting the see-through partition that separated them. Still no response. Valdez stared at the blue helmet. *What's wrong? Why doesn't he speak?*

"Come on," he said. "Talk!"

But, as he shouted, he somehow knew Umbro wouldn't answer. He had a strange sense of being alone. And that's when he froze, trapped in a moment of horror. Everything seemed to stop – his heart, his breathing, his thoughts, his movements. The moment, although only a few seconds, seemed like an age. Then, as his feelings and thoughts slowly came back, he began to understand what was happening.

He, Valdez, was trapped in a shuttle, flying low over newly formed rainforest, on an Earth-cloned planet. Umbro was injured, unconscious . . . or perhaps even dead.

He was trapped in the thunderous, lumbering, clumsy shuttle.

Trapped!

CHAPTER TWO

Valdez did nothing. He looked at the instrument console. He looked around the pod. He flicked at bits of fluff on his coveralls. He was in a daze. This is not happening, he thought. In a moment Umbro will speak to me. But he didn't.

Slowly, Umbro's helmet rolled backwards and forwards. Valdez slapped the partition again, then realised he was being shoved about, too. The shuttle was shaking and jerking again. It was still flying!

How?

Valdez searched the dials, screens and pads for the computer pilot indicator. It wasn't highlighted. The shuttle was still on manual control, but Umbro wasn't flying it. Umbro!

What was wrong? If only he could get to him.

He put his hand on the partition. “Please, Umbro, please wake up!”

The shuttle shook again, then rolled violently. Three or four lights flashed. Valdez looked at the image screen and saw thick green forests. He had to get control of the shuttle. He . . . he had to fly the shuttle . . . somehow.

Ignoring the flashing lights, he scanned the console. So many dials, screens, pads and lights. There. He hit the computer pilot pad. Nothing. A dial scrolling numbers stopped on 1200, scrolled again and stopped on 1100.

Okay. Altitude’s dropping.

Another screen. Another set of numbers: 110, 112, 110, 100, 114, 95 . . . Valdez noticed slight increases and decreases in speed as the numbers changed.

Okay. Speed’s dropping.

Forget the flashing lights. I know the altitude and speed. Test them. He pressed a pad on his armrest. The handheld column popped up. He gripped it and rotated the wheel bar. The shuttle responded and slid left. He eased the column back. On the image screen, the view of the trees shortened and the scrolling numbers dropped to 90.

He pushed the column forward. The numbers rose to 120 and the view of the trees lengthened. He pushed and pulled the column until he was sure he had controlled the altitude and speed, then he locked the column on a level course and sat back. Drops of sweat ran into his eyes. His heart thumped and his hands shook. No time to relax. What next?

He scanned the console again. The flashing lights had stopped. He needed a trip log – something to tell him where he was and where he was going. The pads and panels had many functions, but he had no idea how to activate them.

One by one, he highlighted as many dials, switches, pads and screens as he could, cursing himself for not knowing more about shuttles and how they worked. He should have spent more time on the flying simulator programmes at the space station, instead of following the progress of the experiments and trials of the new habitats on Eco.

In the centre of the console he recognised a pad – the communicator-intercom. He slapped his helmet. Why hadn't he thought of it before?

Had Umbro already used it? Were rescue craft already tracking their limping shuttle? He stabbed the pad with his thumb. His helmet filled with crackling static. Which channel was open? He hit the pad again. The static changed to a quiet hum.

"Hello! This is . . . " What? I don't even know the shuttle's call sign. Umbro did that. "Hello! Hello! This is Valdez . . . and Umbro. Respond, Home Base. We're somewhere in the Eastern Quarter . . . over the rainforest. Something is wrong with Umbro . . . "

He waited and heard nothing, just the quiet hum. Was the communicator working? His heart thumped wildly again. He felt an overwhelming rush of blood to his head and saw spots before his eyes. Panic hit him. He had managed to fight it off while he worked out how to control the shuttle. But now, with the thought that no one knew what was happening, it was back. He hit the communicator pad three times and screamed.

"Home Base! I'm stranded . . . rainforest! The shuttle . . . I've never flown before . . . I can't fly . . . I can't fly!"

He clenched his fists and hit the partition. "Umbro! Home Base! Someone . . ."

But all he heard was the hum, then, ever so faintly some static, followed by a voice. He sat up, straining to hear. The voice faded in and out. He picked up a few broken words: "Reply . . . message . . . rescue". And then the hum was back.

Valdez hit the communicator pad again and spoke quickly. If anyone was receiving his signal, he had to give them as much information as he could. "Umbro and Valdez. Venom shuttle. Observation flight from Home Base. Destination – the new rainforests. Eastern Quarter. Struck by some force. Umbro is unconscious or worse. The shuttle on unknown flight path. I cannot fly. I repeat. I cannot fly."

He waited one, two, three minutes, listening to the hum, desperately hoping to hear the static and the voice again, but there was nothing. He thumped the pod wall.

"Come on! Someone! Please . . ."

Then he had a sudden thought. What if the person he'd heard wasn't on Eco at all. Perhaps some other spacecraft within Eco's star boundaries had picked up his emergency message and was trying to contact him. Again, he hit the pad.

"My name is Valdez. I am a member of Home

Base, Planet Eco. I am a scientist. I am part of the biological team that is developing an Earth-cloned planet. The first immigrants will arrive from Earth within six lunar months. A mysterious virus has struck Eco. The virus threatens Eco's existence. I have information . . . I know . . ."

His voice started to crack. He gritted his teeth then opened his mouth and forced himself to take slow, deep breaths.

"If anyone anywhere can hear me who can help me, respond. Please respond!"

Valdez didn't hear the static or the voice again. For almost an hour, he talked and listened, talked and listened, sending the same message, hoping someone would hear him. As time went on, his doubts grew. Was the communicator working? Had Umbro deactivated it? Was their low-flying altitude affecting reception? What if someone did respond? What could they do? An impossible situation. Hopeless. Or was it? He couldn't give up. He had to do something. But what?

He looked at the console and the screens again. He closed his eyes, trying to remember his time on the simulator. The simulator used a Cobra – a smaller, short-range, two-seater shuttle. He saw the pod in his mind. Two seats, side by side, the instrument console almost identical to the Venom. Had he done a landing or had the computer pilot controlled that? He remembered odd bits about quasi-power thrusters, retractable wings and flaps, hover lift-offs, but it was all vague . . . all so vague. He hit the communicator pad again and repeated his emergency message.

Nothing.

No one could help him.

He felt the fluttering of panic again. He fought it by slowly, carefully speaking aloud. "I'm trapped inside a Venom shuttle. I'm cruising at around 100 macroknots, 1000 maskmetres above Eco. Destination, unknown. Energy reserves, unknown . . . Energy! How long before the shuttle's energy runs out and I crash? Seconds? Minutes? Hours?"

Valdez had to decide. Did he wait and risk landing wherever, or did he start looking for a place to try a controlled landing? He glanced at the thick, green rainforests that filled the image screen. Landing in that would be impossible. The trees would tear the shuttle apart. But then, any landing would be a crash landing. He tried the communicator again. His message was short.

"Emergency! Emergency! Respond!"

Every fifteen minutes or so, he sent out the message. In between, he started to form a plan. He didn't know where he was. He didn't want to wait until there was no energy. He wanted to control where he took the shuttle down. Common sense told him a desert, grasslands, even a swamp would be better than landing in the rainforest. That meant changing course. But would that confuse the rescuers?

"Forget the rescuers," he told himself. "If I was being tracked I would have heard from them. Change course. Find a clear space to land."

Valdez unlocked the control column and eased it forward, feeling the speed increase. He eased the column back and felt the speed decrease.

"Okay," he said. "That's all there is to it. Find a clear space, ease the column forward, take the shuttle down. Then ease the column back. Glide. Ease the column back some more. Slow the shuttle. Land . . . Land. Hah! It sounds so easy."

But he knew it wouldn't be.

Land. How he wished his feet were planted firmly on land.

Again, he tried to imagine what would happen.

Take the shuttle down. Land the shuttle. The crash. There would be a crash. He swallowed hard and pressed a pad below the image screen to widen the view below. Then he rotated the wheel bar on the column and the shuttle began a cycle of wide, sweeping loops.

Staring at the screen, searching for a break in the rainforests, he didn't notice the lights flashing on the console. First green, then yellow. Suddenly, a shrill beeping echoed around him and the lights flashed red. Startled, Valdez heard a computerised voice. "Energy low! Energy low! Pilot override. Emergency landing! Repeat. Emergency landing!"

Valdez twitched the control column. There was no response. The computer pilot now controlled the shuttle. He saw the speed fall to 90 and the altitude drop to 900. The shuttle was going down . . . into the trees. He was going to die . . .

Valdez looked at the console. Almost every light and pad was flashing, but he was searching for one in particular – the one that would give him back control of the shuttle. Which was it?

Speed, 85. Altitude, 850.

Come on, he thought. It's here. It has to be here. Which one? Which one?

Speed, 80. Altitude, 800.

He must be looking in the wrong place. Tens of lights and pads were flashing on the main console but only one light, a green one, was flashing on the control column. It had to be the override. Valdez pressed it. Immediately the lights stopped flashing and all turned yellow. Valdez heard the computerised voice again. "Manual override active. Pilot has control."

He eased the column back. His speed increased and he gained altitude. Then, without warning, there was a loud whoosh of expelled air and the engine hum whirred and died. There was sudden silence. The lights across all the consoles flashed red again. He had no power. The shuttle's energy was exhausted.

Valdez felt the blood drain from his limbs to feed his thumping heart. He had no choice. He pushed the column forward. He was going down.

CHAPTER THREE

He knew he couldn't freeze as he had before. He had to concentrate. Find a space. A space to land. But the screens showed only thick, green trees.

This is it, he thought. This is where it ends. He looked again at Umbro's helmet, flopped to one side. They were both going to die. Somehow he didn't feel frightened. The tight, anxious feeling was still there, but it wasn't overpowering now. The silence helped him think. Shifting in his seat, he edged the column forward again.

He tried to descend slowly, pushing the column further forward when he felt a slow, shuddering stall beginning. All the time, he kept his eyes on the image screen.

Lower.

Lower.

The trees were not as thick as they looked.

Were they thinning out? Perhaps he was nearing a border of the rainforest. Valdez checked the trees again. He was sure they were getting smaller and shorter. He had to be close to a forest border.

He took a couple of deep breaths. New hope had made him nervous again.

Yes!

There.

What was that?

He halted the cycle of wide, sweeping loops and steered the shuttle into a straight-line descent. Something amid the green. What was it? A colour change. Yes. Just a flash. He flicked the column left and right, weaving the shuttle.

Yes!

To the left.

He brought the shuttle back that way and saw the edge of the forest. It stopped suddenly before a gap – a space of about 700 minimetres long and 400 wide. Then the forest grew again beyond the gap. What was the gap? Valdez centred the image screen on it. The ground looked solid. Something was glinting. Water? He could land on water.

Speed, 100 macroknots. Altitude, 1200 maskmetres.

Speed's increased. Keep it steady. Not too fast. Not too slow. Somewhere around 70 macroknots seemed about right. Now, get the shuttle on a landing path for the gap.

He jiggled the column. Nothing happened. He pulled hard to the left. Slowly, oh, so slowly, the shuttle came round. Valdez held the column there until the gap came on to the screen. It looked far away. And there was definitely liquid.

Eco's crust was similar to Earth's – a mixture of metals, minerals and water – so there wasn't any danger of toxins. And was that vegetation in the gap, too? Not green, but browns, yellows, oranges and black. Sharp ridges and small gullies had also appeared. And steam, or was it smoke? Eco also had many open wounds that oozed or spat steam, water, gas, mud and lava. Perhaps the gap was a volcanic vent. A volcanic rock vent. That would explain why there were no trees.

Can't land on solid rock.

Pull up.

Won't respond.

Too late.

Altitude, 600 maskmetres. Speed, 90 macroknots.

Too fast.

Everything looked close enough to touch. Trees, rocky ground, yellow streaks. Was that sulphur? A shadow. A moving shadow.

An animal.

Then the rock gap was under him and everything happened at once.

He jiggled the column. No control.

He let go.

He heard the screaming wrench as parts of the fuselage were ripped free. He hadn't cleared the trees. He crossed his arms, leaned forward and braced himself. Glancing at the screen, he saw the shuttle hadn't been knocked off course. Then a monstrous thump knocked the wind out of him. He smelt scorched ceramics then heard an explosion. He was slammed back in his seat, then he had an unusual sensation of spinning, freefalling, flying. It felt as if his pod had come away from the shuttle. Somewhere in the distance, he heard grinding, wrenching, tearing, squealing, thumping – and an almighty smash.

Then he was rolling and crashing, as if he were inside a huge ball being flicked about, wrenched from side to side before finally coming to rest.

Valdez opened his eyes. There was light. He was still inside the pod but upside down. He saw rocks – red, orange, yellow rocks – with steam escaping from between them, and mud, flat-leafed plants and more mud. Where was the partition? Where was Umbro's helmet? Where was Umbro? Then everything went black.

CHAPTER FOUR

A flashback.

The betrayal.

His memory was so clear he heard his sneakers squeaking on the tile floors as he ran along the corridor towards the restricted labs.

The labs were being used for experiments with growth accelerants. Newly discovered minerals deep in the Moon's core were known to accelerate plant growth – incredible growth. In just thirty-six hours, any plant fed with the new liquid mineral mixture would grow fruit. As soon as the fruit was picked, the plant turned to seed, died and decomposed.

The development of the accelerants was very exciting. They would help feed Earth's population explosion and they would also be used on all new plants on the cloned planets. The fast-growing plants would also speed up the new planets' oxygen production.

Valdez was late. He was supposed to be videologging the plants, counting the fruit, noting any differences in stem and leaf structure. He had run all the way from the dormitory, passed his palm over the identity scanner outside Lab 02. When the doors slicked open, he hurried along the rows of climbing plants to the technology centre. There, he grabbed one of the finger videos and pulled the small elastic machine over his hand. It looked like a glove, but when Valdez pointed it at a plant, it took many readings – photos, temperature, length, height, weight measurements, acid and alkaline levels and water content. The information was fed straight into Eco's master computers.

Valdez moved down the first row of plants, running his hand across the leaves, stems, fruits and flowers.

He heard voices.

Usually the senior scientists didn't come into the labs until after they'd read the morning's new data and Valdez had only just started. He moved towards the voices, then stopped when he realized it was Sera and Umbro. They were arguing. He had stayed among the thick foliage and listened, but only managed to catch a few words.

"You must!" insisted Umbro.

Silence.

"No," said Sera. "It's too dangerous."

Then Umbro again. "Not dangerous, but safer. It will . . . you leave me no choice. In the next few days . . . I will get it . . ."

Betrayal.

Valdez opened his eyes. His head throbbed. He shook it, making the ache worse. Where was he? The crash. The shuttle was down. He had landed in a strange cut of ground between thick clumps of trees. He was still inside the pod.

Ejected? He must have been shot out of the shuttle before it crashed.

The pod was still moving, manoeuvring itself into a vertical position. That was what had woken him. Slowly, he came upright. Late afternoon light flooded the small space. He shut his eyes to stop the glare. The pod shook, wrenched, then finally settled and the clear cover above him opened.

Immediately, Valdez heard strange sounds.

Rustling, hissing, gurgling.

Valdez unhooked his harness, pushed himself upwards, felt a sharp pain in his elbow and slumped down. Slowly, he tried again and managed to ease himself up on to the seat headrest. He pulled off his helmet and suddenly remembered that Eco's atmosphere was newly oxygenated and very few people had been outdoors without an air suit. He held his breath, then took in small gasps. He didn't feel dizzy, or breathless.

He breathed deeper and noticed the air tasted slightly sweet. Was that normal? Then he noticed the rustling was wind, the hissing was steam escaping from a vent in the rock beside the pod and the gurgling was hot, plopping mud.

The new sounds were suddenly interrupted by tearing, wrenching metal and ceramics. Further along the rocky strip, he saw the Venom's nose grinding against the rough rocks. It was upright, but sinking slowly into swampy mud.

Valdez scrambled out of the pod, leaped down and collapsed on the ground. Every bone in his body screamed. His head spun. He didn't know if it was lack of oxygen or the shock of the crash. He stayed down on his hands and knees and waited for his head to clear, then got to his feet slowly and staggered towards the Venom. It was sinking fast. He ran again, awkwardly, clumsily. But it was too late. The nose slid into the swamp and disappeared amid the sound of sloppy sucking.

"Umbro!"

Where was Umbro? Had he been ejected from the shuttle or was he still trapped inside?

He spun round. Too quickly. Sharp pain ripped through his head again. He saw white, hot lights, collapsed to his knees, his bones jarring on the hard rocks. He tried to get up but couldn't. He rested his head on his arms and everything went black again.

It was dark when Valdez woke up – dark and silent, except for the soft plopping of mud and the hissing of steam.

Night.

And he was alone.

Umbro.

There was no sign of him. Valdez got to his feet. His head didn't throb so much now, but his legs and arms ached terribly. He looked around, but it was too dark to see anything. Pitch black. He tried to work out where the steam vents and hot, muddy pools were or where the rocks ended and the swamp began.

"Umbro," he called softly.

Then louder. "Umbro!" His voice bounced off the rocks and was swallowed by the trees. There was no answer. Valdez dropped to the rocks. "Where is Umbro?"

He rubbed his arm and felt a lump, then ran his hands over the rest of his body but found nothing strained or broken. I've been lucky, he thought. I survived the crash with no injuries.

Lucky?

Sera's betrayal. The spreading virus. The crash. Umbro missing. Alone. That's luck? Yes, a whole lot of bad luck.

He sighed. Don't think like that, he told himself. You could be dead, but you're alive.

Alive.

That's got to be good.

Good luck.

He shifted on the rock and felt its warmth. Pressing his hands over it, he felt the rock getting warmer as the sound of hissing steam got louder.

He crawled around, feeling all the rocks. Close to the forest, the rock surface was almost icy cold. The rock must be being warmed by underground heated water moving towards the steam vent.

He crawled back to the warm spot and sat facing where he'd last seen the shuttle. He could see the grey outline of the thick vegetation around the swamp and the trees beyond that. The sky was lightening. With luck, it would be morning soon.

Now he could hear a rhythmic buzzing – soft, but slowly getting louder. It was an insect sound – a clicking and buzzing. Then something tugged his hair. But it was still dark.

His eyes snapped open. It wasn't dark. It was light. He must have dozed off. He sat up and found himself surrounded by tiny, blue-green creatures, buzzing and clicking. He slapped them away, but there were too many. They dived at him, grabbing his hair in their tiny limbs and ripping the strands free. Valdez yelped and squealed, slapping himself now, but the swarm blanketed him. They grabbed larger clumps of hair and ripped it free. As they tugged his hair, they squirted his face with spray, making his skin itch but Valdez couldn't scratch because he was too busy waving his arms. He scrambled to his feet and wrapped his arms over his head, but the creatures crawled into the creases in his coveralls and burrowed under his arms. He spun around, yelling, "Get off! Get away!"

Then he remembered his helmet. It was lying on the ground beside the pod. Keeping his arms wrapped around his head, he stumbled towards it and jammed it on his head, making sure all loose hair was tucked safely inside. Then, as quickly as they had arrived, the creatures disappeared. They swarmed away over the swamp, zipped among some reed-like plants and began stripping fine, wispy strands from the leaves. Amazed, Valdez watched them, still hurting from the attack. He might have expected biting or stinging creatures, but not hair-pullers.

The sun was coming up. Valdez stood and faced it, feeling it warm his face. Carefully, he took off the helmet, but held on to it in case the odd little creatures returned. He ran his fingers through his tangled hair. The creatures had probably only ripped out a few strands, but it felt like a whole lot more. His face was tender, lumpy and itchy in the places where he'd been sprayed. He wanted to scratch the lumps, but guessed that that would only make them bleed or blister.

His body still ached. He raised his arms and stretched, trying to ease the stiffness and looked around. His head hurt, but nowhere near as badly as the day before. He was standing on what seemed to be a volcanic rock plateau. The shuttle had come down in one of the few places in the forest where there was a break in the vegetation.

Lucky again?

Perhaps.

The ground was rocky, swampy and dotted with steaming vents. The rocks were ridged and stained yellow and orange from the hot mineral water. Valdez walked to the edge of the plateau. There were many types of plants and trees here. Small bushes grew below taller, wide-leaved trees, which in turn were dwarfed by huge, thicktrunked giants that towered out of sight. Many of the trees were tangled with wrist-thick vines that twined in and around the trunks and branches. The vegetation looked dense, but Valdez reckoned he could move through it if he had to.

He wandered back towards the pod, scanning the swamp where the Venom had disappeared.

The shuttle had smashed all the taller, thick-trunked trees, leaving the long, broad-leaved reeds, which seemed to move about on their own. Valdez was sure they had been in a different pattern when he'd looked before. Perhaps he could step on to them from a rocky ledge. There might be all sorts of things from the shuttle lying about in the swamp. Valdez stretched out his foot to test the closest clump. When it sank into oozy brown mud, he shook his head.

So.

Here he was.

In the wild.

Alone.

It was weird. Not many hours ago, he had been in the most highly advanced biological laboratory in the known universe. And now he was trapped in the wilderness on a brand new planet with a virus that was destroying all oxygen-making vegetation. It was as if he were in an ancient, twenty-first century video diary. Valdez couldn't remember ever being alone, and the last time he'd been in the wilderness was back on Earth, which seemed a lifetime ago.

He shook his head. His headache was back – a

sharp thumping just above his eyes. He wandered to the edge of the forest and sat down in a naturally curved rock seat that fitted his body perfectly.

Tired.

So tired.

It was then he noticed other noises – creature noises. Not buzzing and clicking, but short, strident cackles and chirps and long, shrill whistles. At another time, he would have found out what creature made each noise. After he rested, he might just do that. He hoped there would be time before the rescuers arrived. They must be on their way. Probably not far away at all.

Yes.

He leaned back, felt the rock's heat warm his back and fell asleep.

CHAPTER FIVE

Valdez came to slowly, dreamily. The crash was running through his mind – the shuttle hitting the trees. He sat up, startled, blinked, rubbed his eyes and looked around. What is this place? Then everything came back. He had crash-landed. The swamp had swallowed the shuttle. Umbro was missing. No, perhaps he was still trapped in the shuttle. If he was, then he was dead for sure.

Dead.

Eco was supposed to be about life – new life for people from overcrowded Earth. But the virus had changed that. Eco's perfect world had been mangled, just like the shuttle.

Valdez got to his feet and stretched his arms and legs carefully. His elbow still ached and his head throbbed a little, but he felt better.

The sun was high in the sky. Its weird, hazy,

reddish glow was the only difference between Earth and Eco. Sera said it had to do with Eco's position in the solar system. Eco was closer to Mars. At different times during the day, the sun scattered Mars' red glow on to Eco.

Valdez licked his dry lips and suddenly felt thirsty. When was the last time he'd had something to drink? Probably before he had left Home Base. He needed to find water.

He walked to the edge of the swamp. The swamp was wet, but the dirty, brackish water was no good for drinking. He knew there was underground water, but the streams flowing from high ground also probably fed the swamp. He turned and walked to the western edge of the plateau, where a hollow in the rock ran all the way to the swamp – a good collection area.

He was so busy searching that he didn't notice the sun disappearing behind thick, dark clouds – large, black, water-heavy clouds, rolling upwards. A flash of lightning suddenly made his hair stand up. Valdez ducked, but the following thunderous thump and boom sucked up the air around him and knocked him to the ground. He went down hard, scraping his hands and elbows and knees, sending more pain shooting through his body. Another flash, another thump, another boom. Then a noise – loud and powerful. It was building, building until it became a roar – a faroff roar that swooped over the trees, across the plateau and attacked him.

Wind.

Roaring, whistling, screeching wind, filled with rain. Hot, heavy drops of rain that thrashed him. But Valdez didn't care. It was water. He stood up and opened his mouth, collecting, swallowing and almost grinning at the pure, wet sweetness of it. Then he remembered that he needed to collect it, too.

A container?

His helmet.

He ran to the curved rock, but just as quickly as they had arrived, the clouds, wind and rain disappeared again. The sun came out and wet, steamy mist and thousands of buzzing, clicking, hair-pulling creatures filled the air. They went straight for Valdez.

He grabbed the helmet, jammed it on his head and crouched with hands and arms over his head waiting for the sun to burn off the steam. He was sure the heat storms probably happened two or three times a day, so he'd always have water.

The hair-pullers were soon gone and Valdez took off the helmet. Sweating in the steamy heat, he undid the clasps on the top half of his coveralls, carefully slipped his arms out of the sleeves, then tied them around his waist.

What now?

Do a check, he told himself. Go over everything. Establish some sort of order of events. The rescue team will want details.

I was aboard a Venom shuttle with Umbro. There was a malfunction, an electrical strike of some sort that injured him, killed him. No, don't think that. Umbro's here somewhere. Probably close by. Perhaps wondering where I am.

Stop.

Go back.

Start the check again – slowly, carefully.

I'm Valdez. I am trapped in the Eastern Quarter of the rainforest habitat . . .

He nodded then went on.

I was aboard a Venom shuttle on an observation flight. There was a blinding flash of light and I was ejected from the shuttle. The shuttle crashed and sank into the swamp. Umbro is injured. His whereabouts is . . . unknown . . . That's it.

Now wait. Yes, wait for the rescuers. There will be a rescue. There has to be. Umbro is important . . . no, he's crucial for solving the virus problem. So, at this moment there are rescue teams exploring the rainforest. Umbro will have logged in the trip details. When trouble struck, he would have contacted Home Base. The crash would have set off the emergency locator transmitter. The rescuers will come today . . . sometime. I will hear them first, then see them. They'll probably arrive in one of the small Ranger craft that use bodyheat- seeking sensors. They'll find me first then they'll find Umbro.

Simple.

Of course it will be simple. Computers control Eco's environment. Many of them are fixed on satellites in space. Right now, someone at Home Base is looking at pictures of the rock plateau, the swamp and me. All I have to do is wait. And, while I wait, I can find out something about this area – something that will be useful to all scientists. And perhaps I'll find something to eat.

Food.

His stomach rumbled. It felt hollow. He hadn't eaten anything since he left Home Base. How long ago was that? One day? Two? He was ravenous.

He thought of the vegetables in the growing houses at Home Base. All the trials were complete. When the new immigrants arrived, they would grow their own food. Just vegetables, though. There had been problems with the many introduced animals, including the sheep, cattle, deer, goats and fish. They had developed mutations and diseases. The new immigrants would bring their own supplies of protein – dehydrated, powdered, liquefied – to nourish them until the animal genetics were sorted out.

Fresh vegetables had made a difference to meals at Home Base. For years everyone had eaten replacement pastes and dry food mixtures. Taste, for Home Base inhabitants, wasn't important until after the harvest of the first crop of vegetables. Now, hardly anyone ate the processed food.

The thought of luscious, dark red tomatoes, crispy green lettuces, juicy yellow corn and multigrained breads just made the rumbling in Valdez's stomach worse.

He sat in the curved rock, letting the sun warm him while he waited. Trying to keep his mind off food, he remembered the survival classes he'd been part of back at Home Base. They were compulsory activities, planned to prepare all inhabitants for living and surviving in the natural environment. Now that the environment had steady oxygen levels, a few people were beginning to explore the outdoors without air suits.

Valdez looked around. He liked being outdoors. He felt free. The last time he'd been in a natural environment was years ago, on Earth, and even then he had worn an air suit and face mask for protection from the acid air.

The survival classes were really just common knowledge – some map reading, first aid and risk management. It was interesting. What was it the instructor said? Know your situation. Identify everything that may be useful. Ignore anything you have no control over.

Okay, thought Valdez, what's my situation? What's useful? He stood up and emptied out his pockets. A useless daily organiser. Nothing else? He patted his coveralls again and felt something solid in one of the leg pockets. Umbro's ceramic and metal tool. He took it out and opened each tool – blade, screwdriver, awl, pick and scissors.

He ran his finger along the knife blade. Deadly sharp. It could be useful. Then he flipped open the organiser and yesterday's Home Base menu scrolled across the screen – bread, tomatoes, oatmeal, corn fritters. He groaned and slammed it shut. The hollow feeling in his stomach deepened. He jammed the knife and organiser back into his pocket. He had to get food.

What had the instructor said about getting food in the wild? Something about exploring the surroundings. Well, there was the swamp, the mud-pools, the sulphur and steam vents and the forest. The only place he hadn't been was the forest. There had to be food there – berries, fruit, nuts, even roots. If he found them, he could eat.

He wandered along the fringe of the forest, not wanting to go in too deep in case the rescuers arrived, but his complaining stomach got the better of him. He pushed through the soft green branches and realised he'd never been in real forest before. It enveloped him, wrapped its cool arms around him, then suddenly exploded with noise.

Valdez jumped and crashed back to the plateau. When the noises faded away, he stepped carefully back into the forest and heard the beating wings of insects and animals, and their clicking legs, snapping jaws and squawking. Were they warning noises or welcoming noises? Once again, he was reminded of how ignorant he was. He enjoyed the fresh air and the open spaces but everything else was confusing. There were so many unknowns in the wilderness. Like the forest around him, he was totally green and raw.

And still hungry.

He stood in the shade, just off the edge of the plateau. A bright picture of a warm, sweet, lightly toasted corn fritter was imprinted on his mind. He shook his head, trying to get rid of it and thought about the rescuers. A small seed of doubt was growing. Valdez knew Umbro hadn't kept to the preset flight course. They had flown low, searching for the virus. They had twisted, turned, veered and looped. And then, when he had taken over the controls, he had taken them further off course, trying to find a landing space in the forest. It didn't make sense.

He shrugged. So, the rescuers might not come

today. Then he had a terrible thought. What if they didn't find him at all? For a moment, fear overcame his hunger. He pushed it away, repeating the survival instructor's words – ignore anything you have no control over.

Okay, so the rescuers might take a little longer than expected. But they would come. He was sure of it. Umbro was too important to Eco's future. He believed they would come for him.

Forget that. Right now, what's most important?

Food.

Valdez looked at the sky. The sun had dropped in behind the trees, casting long shadows across the landscape. He could hear the clicking and buzzing building again as the sun dropped further in the sky. He hurried back to the curved rock and grabbed his helmet. He would be ready for the hair-pullers this time.

"Food," he said to himself. "I have to find something to eat, then somewhere to sleep. Yes. Food and shelter. That's what the instructor said. Survival depends on good food and shelter."

CHAPTER SIX

Valdez sat with his arms around his head. The hair-pullers buzzed and snapped and sprayed him. He ignored them, trying to remember everything he'd heard and seen in the survival classes. He was glad he'd been interested, because those few short hours each week were now vitally important.

The instructor had put it to them like this: "You are in the wilderness. Your food supplies run out. What do you do?"

"Look for food from the environment," someone had said.

That night, the group had been in one of the plant research domes – a huge indoor cloche – that had thick-stemmed, flat-leaved and fatfruited plants.

"Although many of these plants have fruit, not all of them can be eaten," said the instructor.

"Your task is to find the plants that can be eaten."

Everyone looked at one another for a moment then one or two nodded as their scientific minds tackled the problem. They had decided not to try any food until they were sure it wasn't poisonous, but without lab equipment that wasn't easy.

Then Valdez had noticed that some of the plants had more bugs feeding on their fruit than others, and, when he looked closer, he saw that the plants with the most bugs also smelled sweet.

"Are the safest wild food plants the ones with animals feeding on them?" he'd asked.

The instructor had nodded. "It's not failsafe but it is an excellent guide, especially if there are many different animals feeding on the plant."

After making sure none was poisonous, Valdez had found the activity fun. He and the others had tasted many fruits, shoots and leaves. Some were bitter, sour and slimy, but a few were sweet, juicy and delicious.

Valdez peered out from under his arms. The plateau was completely shaded and the hairpullers were gone. He figured he had about an hour before it was dark – an hour to find food. He stood up, but too quickly. He stumbled. His head spun. He closed his eyes and waited for it to clear, impatiently. A day and a half, almost two days without food. That's why he was lightheaded. He moved back to the fringe of the forest and pushed his way into the foliage.

If I could just reach out and grab something, anything, to eat the way I do back at Home Base, he thought, what would I have? Sausages, sauce, hamburgers, cake, chocolate, ice cream, doughnuts. I'd have the lot.

He stopped and leaned against a tree. Thinking of all that tasty food made his mouth wet and his legs weak. He had to stop thinking about Home Base food. None of it was here.

Through the leaves and branches, he could still see the plateau, but only just. I won't go any deeper, he thought, and began to search. Among the mass of greenery, he wanted to see berries – tiny splashes of blue, red and yellow – but there was nothing.

What had the instructor said? Don't look up. Look down. Or was it the other way round? Valdez couldn't see anything when he looked up, so he crouched down, ran his hands through the damp leaf litter and grinned. There were berries there –

soft, squishy, overripe purple berries. Look down, then look up. That's what the instructor had said. Often there are traces of berries, nuts and seeds that birds have dropped or are feeding on.

Valdez stood up and peered into the trees. He could see berries growing on leafy branches, but they were too high. He'd have to climb to reach them and he didn't have the strength for that. He moved on.

Now he saw berries all over the forest floor. They were dirty but they teased him. They seemed to be saying, "Here I am. Come on. Eat me."

Valdez couldn't stop himself. He picked up a couple and blew on them, brushed away the dirt, then nibbled. Sweet. Definitely a berry taste, but also gritty. Was that the dirt or the tiny seeds inside? If he ate more fallen berries, he'd have to wash them first. He shook his head. It was getting much darker in the forest. Not enough time.

He moved on again, hoping to find berries on lower bushes, or perhaps some nuts or seeds. Bird movements seemed to be getting busier, too. He hadn't noticed them before but, even in the fading light, their plumage – bright oranges, greens, blues, yellows and pinks – stood out. They had come down from their higher perches for a final feed at the end of the day. Valdez saw webbed feet and feet with talons, flat and pointed beaks, long and short legs, but all of them had small, stumpy wings that beat furiously as they manoeuvred in and around the thick foliage.

He almost missed it – a small, flattened bush with light, waxy leaves and hairy clumps around the roots. Flitting into the middle of the bush were tiny birds, no bigger than his palm, with large red eyes and minuscule wings beating fast and furious. Each bird came out of the bush carrying a blue, curly frond in its beak, which it took to a higher branch, stripped small beads off the stem and ate.

Valdez watched the birds fluttering back and forth until his rumbling stomach forced him forward. The birds scattered, chirping noisily. He reached into the centre of the bush, snapped off a blue frond and smelt it. Sweet. He took a nibble and a small explosion of syrupy sugar filled his mouth. He pushed it into his mouth, chomped twice and swallowed. He tasted the sweetness all the way to his stomach. It was exquisite.

Now, nothing could stop him. He went quickly

from bush to bush, grabbing fronds and stuffing them into his mouth, munching and crunching them. Blue juice dribbled from his chin. What was the taste? Something he knew. Sort of like sweets, chewing gum, jelly, jam and marshmallow, all mixed together. He knew he should eat slowly, but he couldn't. His hunger was too strong. After two days without food, there was a big hole to fill. But he felt full surprisingly quickly. He slowed his eating, then collected more fronds.

When his pockets were full, he pushed his way out on to the plateau, where he could just make out the shape of the pod beside the swamp in the fading light. He moved quickly before total blackness surrounded him.

By the time he reached the curved rock, he was exhausted again. His legs felt weak and the small, nagging ache above his eyes was back. He needed to remember he was still getting over the crash. He mustn't do too much too quickly.

He shook the fronds out of his pockets and dropped them into a shallow hole in a rock, then covered the hole with a flat stone to keep them safe from animals. He knew he had to find a better place to sleep. The rock was too hard and too exposed, but for the moment he just wanted to rest.

The fronds were churning in his stomach. He had had this feeling once before, a long time ago on Earth when he'd eaten too many unripe apples. Had he eaten too many fronds? He didn't think so. It was probably just his starved system getting used to food again.

Now, shelter. He knew nothing about building shelter. The instructor had only mentioned the word and explained what it was.

A shelter will need to protect me from the sun, the wind and the rain, he thought. The rescuers will come to the plateau, so it has to be close by – perhaps in the fringe of the forest. The land there is flat and thick with plenty of vegetation, so I should be able to build one. It can't be that hard.

He shifted in the hollow rock and noticed the pod again. What about that as a shelter? It's small and it can be sealed, which will protect me from the rain, wind and wandering animals or bugs. Perhaps if I drag it away from the edge of the swamp, set it in a place where it will stay upright, it would be okay for sleeping.

He pushed himself out of the hollow rock

and walked stiffly over to the pod. The hatch was open. It had locked in place when the portable energy pack ran out, but he was sure, once he was inside, he could force it shut.

He leaned on the pod, grabbed the lip of the hatch and pulled hard, dragging it away from the swamp. After five or six steps, he stopped. Quick, sharp pains tightened his stomach. He waited until they passed, then pulled the pod again, scraping, squealing, screeching on the rocks, and wedged it into a small hollow. He leaned on the pod to make sure it didn't roll forwards or backwards. It wobbled a bit, but he couldn't move it any further. He was exhausted and the stomach pains had worsened. Now he was worried. Were the fronds poisonous? He knew he shouldn't have eaten so many so quickly.

He climbed into the pod and stretched out. The pains eased a little. He shifted to get comfortable and felt dampness soak through his coveralls. The seat was still wet from the afternoon rain. He reached up and tugged the hatch closed. He was just able to hear the hissing and blooping of the steam and mud. The stars above him blinked and winked. He fell asleep, silently wishing, "Please, come soon . . . Please."

CHAPTER SEVEN

Sera! Sera!" His eyes snapped open. Pitch black. Where am I? He pushed himself up in his seat and remembered Sera. And he remembered Umbro. Both of them in the laboratory, talking quietly, not knowing he was listening. The sharp words.

Umbro saying he knew.

Sera saying she didn't care. It was too late. The damage was done. No going back.

Umbro asking for something.

Sera laughing – a weird, high-pitched laugh he had never heard before – then shaking her head and saying forget it. You'll never have it.

Then Umbro rushing out of the lab and Sera not moving, just standing quite still, watching the closed door. Thinking. Thinking. Thinking what?

A few moments later, she had left, too, and Valdez realised he'd been holding his breath. He let it out slowly, trying to work out what they'd been talking about.

Valdez was brought back to the present by a sudden hot flush that raced over his body, forcing him to scratch and itch. He rubbed his arms, his legs, his stomach, back and head, but the itch got worse. It felt as if his body was alive with thousands of tiny creatures just below the skin, all wriggling and twisting and wrestling to break through the surface.

Get out of the pod. Get the coveralls off.

He thrust the hatch back and stumbled out on to the rocks, just as the sooty sky was ripped apart by lightning. A thundering boom followed, which drove him to his knees again. Then the clouds burst and in seconds he was drenched – but a cooling drench that soaked his fiery body. He didn't take shelter. He stripped to the waist and let the heavy, wet drops cool him some more. The lightning and thunder reminded him of Sera and Umbro again.

What could they have been arguing about? An experiment? A procedure? A mistake? No. Nothing so simple. Sera had had something that Umbro wanted, but she'd refused to give it to him. Why?

A couple of days later, all Eco residents had been ordered to assemble in the great hall for the first time since Valdez arrived on Eco. He thought the meeting was for final information about the immigrants, but when he entered the hall he had sensed a dark mood. No talk. No laughter. And no one had looked at him. Everyone had stared at Eco's commander standing on the stage with Sera and Umbro beside her. Umbro had looked worried, but Sera was calm, with a tiny smile at the corner of her mouth.

Then the commander had told them about the mystery virus and how it had infected the rainforest habitat and was expected to spread to the grasslands. After nodding at Sera and Umbro, she went on. An antidote had been produced. It was in its final trial stages. But, if it wasn't successful, then the immigrants would be sent back to Earth and Eco would be quarantined.

"Sera!" he screamed into the night again. And the night thundered back.

He dragged his cooled body back inside the pod, fell into the wet, squelchy seat and slept.

He came around slowly as if he were crawling out of a deep hole. Feelings of dread, hunger, thirst and loneliness almost overwhelmed him. What was going to happen? Why hadn't the rescue team found him? Their technology – heat-seeking sensors, emergency transmitter signals, tracking data, satellite images – should lead them right to the plateau. But it hadn't. He opened his eyes, fighting the feeling of hopelessness. Shifting in the pod, he felt his aches and pains again. The small, cramped space was no good as a shelter. He had to find something better.

Shelter.

I have to keep myself busy, he thought. I have to find somewhere dry and warm or make something dry and warm where I can be comfortable.

The sun poured through the hatch cover. He was sweating now. He looked down at his body and was shocked to see masses of purplish-red welts. He remembered the fierce itchiness he'd felt in the night and then the rain easing it. But what had caused it? The sweet fronds? He picked a couple out of his pocket and smelt them. Sweeter. They must have been unripe when he ate them before. He shook his head. It was hot inside the pod, irritating the welts, making him want to scratch them.

Valdez clambered on to the rocks and pulled the coveralls back over his shoulders. The damp, cool material immediately eased the itching.

Day three. Shelter day.

The lonely feeling was still there. Hunger was part of it. Geez, he was hungry. He had to find more food. Different food. He ate the last of the leftover fronds slowly, chewing them to mush before swallowing. They were sweeter, but they made him thirsty.

Water, food and shelter. He shook his head, amazed again at how important they were.

Water first.

He walked into the forest. The day before, he'd seen some large-leaved, low-slung trees that had water sitting in hollows where the branches met the trunk. Thirty paces in, he found one. It had a big, bulb-like trunk with four main branches. Each branch had a pool of clear, cool water near the trunk. Valdez flicked away a few swimming insects from the closest hollow, then cupped and dipped his hands into the liquid and slurped it up. The cold water cramped his stomach.

Small sips, he told himself. Take small sips.

The water made him feel less hungry, but he knew that wouldn't last. He walked on, searching for the blue frond trees. The sun in the east, filtering through the forest, dappled the limbs and leaves. The birds seemed quieter than they had last evening. He stopped to watch a few and saw some hanging nests. They were ball-shaped and woven carefully from what looked like fine, pale strands of reed. The strands were so fine they looked like hair.

Hoping to find eggs inside, Valdez knocked one to the ground. No eggs, but there was a swarm of hair-pullers. They rushed up from the nest, buzzed around his head and clung to his hair. He swatted them away easily. The cool, dark conditions made them less active. Now he knew why the little creatures attacked him. His long hair was perfect for their elaborate nests.

Valdez moved on. He kept his head down, searching for some colour that might be a sign of food up above. When he stopped, it wasn't for something he saw, but something he felt – something that made the hairs on the back of his neck stand up.

A sound. He stopped and listened. Something was moving just like him, brushing past trees, slapping branches, squelching in soft mud.

Umbro!

But Valdez didn't move. He didn't make a sound. He stood still, waiting, his breath short and shallow, his heart thumping.

Umbro. Please, let it be Umbro.

But instinct told him it wasn't. The sounds, the movements were too big, too heavy, too clumsy.

Right there.

My God! It was huge. An ape-like creature. White. Yellow dorsal spines and a head horn. Heavy arms with taloned fingers that swept across the bushes, grabbing at some reddish leaf pods. The creature had handfuls of the pods, which it squeezed and burst, sending a shower of orange nuts into its upturned mouth. The creature moved quickly, its eyes fixed on the swollen-leaved bushes – grabbing, squeezing and eating. Valdez watched it. He saw stumpy, grinding teeth that could easily crush any of his limbs and silently wished for the creature to be gone.

It was right there. Twenty paces away, moving on a parallel path. Valdez smelt it. A musty, dusty, damp, wet clothes smell. All it had to do was look up and it would see him. But it didn't. It was too busy feeding. Rolling, lumbering, snuffling, it gradually moved on, deeper into the forest.

Seconds, then a minute later and still Valdez hadn't moved. He stayed still, straining his ears until all he heard was the soft twittering of lowflying, yellow-feathered birds feeding on the bits of spilled food left by the creature.

Now Valdez moved. Further into the forest in the opposite direction to the creature. Slowly at first, then jogging, then running, ducking and swerving, brushing any low branches aside. As he ran, he let out a low groan that had all his trapped fear inside it. Puffing, out of breath, with his legs aching again, he had to slow down, then stop.

He sank to his knees and gasped, shaking his head. The creature was a monster. What was it? It had to be one of the malformed, cloned creatures from their failed animal experiments. A hybrid of some sort. All Eco animals were non-aggressive, but Valdez couldn't be sure that that trait hadn't also been mixed up. The thought of the scrunched, squashed face with large, square-blocked teeth made him shiver all over again.

He was starting to hate this place. He didn't want to be here. He was a Home Base, laboratory, dormitory kind of guy, not a jungle dweller.

The creature. Had it seen him, sensed him and ignored him because it had gone to warn others? Were there others? By crashing through the trees, had he made his whereabouts known? He held his breath and listened again.

Nothing.

With luck, the creature was alone and roaming and would be long gone by nightfall.

Feeling a bit calmer, Valdez looked carefully at the bushes the creature had been feeding on. He picked a pod, squeezed it in his hand and caught the orange nuts that bounced free. He smelt them. Salty. He licked them. Very salty. He took a bite and chewed. Nutty and tasty. He collected a handful of pods, broke them open and dropped three or four nuts into his mouth. Just a few at a time, he reminded himself. If there were no sudden bad effects, then he'd have a few more in an hour or two.

He moved on a short way, found a frond bush and made sure he collected the overripe ones. Mixed with the nuts, they'd make a good meal.

He had water. He had food. And now for the shelter. He headed back the way he'd come, following the creature's trail of broken branches, shredded leaves and empty nut pods. He walked slowly, filling his pockets with more nuts. Every now and then, he stopped to listen to the sounds of the forest, but only heard the soft flittering, squeaking and whistling of birds, mixed in with the clicking, buzzing and snapping of insects.

Then, not fifty paces from the hollow rock, he heard rustling in the undergrowth again. He froze and crouched, ready to run. About ten paces directly in front of him, the lower bushes shook and a family of four rabbit-like animals – grey fur, short tails, floppy ears – waddled out into the open, then disappeared beneath another bush. Valdez let out a sigh. He dropped his hands to his knees to stop them shaking.

It's okay, he told himself. It's not the monster.

They're harmless. Move on ... Come on, move.

Slowly, quietly, he forced himself to place one foot in front of the other until he was past the low bushes. Then he ran, not stopping until he burst out on to the plateau beside the hollow rock. He was worn out again, but he couldn't stop, wouldn't stop until he had some sort of shelter.

He emptied the nuts and fruit fronds from his pockets into the shallow hole then covered it again with the flat rock.

The shelter.

It would be in the forest, but not far from the plateau.

He decided to pick four points – four large trees along the forest fringe – and walk fifty paces from them into the forest to search for a good site. If he found nothing, he would carry on picking more search points until he was successful.

He was lucky again.

On his third search, about fifty paces from the plateau, the ground suddenly rose up. It was some sort of upright rock formation that looked like an outpouring of lava – a porous peak three times as high as Valdez and at least fifteen paces across. He'd only seen it because it had blocked his way. The rocky face was hidden behind foliage and the crown disappeared into the treetops. While looking up, Valdez was sure he saw shadows across the face.

Caves?

He moved across and around the base, pulling

greenery away. There were natural bumps and cracks that fitted his hands and feet. He jammed his boots into two deep cracks. Then, hand over hand, he pulled himself up slowly. About three body lengths off the ground, he scrambled on to a smooth ledge. The ledge went back into the rock and formed a natural roof. He didn't need to climb any further. The cave, about eight paces across and six paces deep, was perfect.

A perfect shelter.

Breathing hard from the climb, Valdez sat on the ledge and rested. This isn't luck, he thought. Luck didn't help me find this cave. I did it on my own. I could be down on the plateau, still wishing for my rescuers to arrive, but I'm not. I'm up here in a new shelter. If I'm going to be here longer than I want to, then I need to adapt. I have to make my own luck.

He looked around.

Yes. With bedding, water and food supplies, this will make a good shelter. He slid his legs over the ledge and eased himself down the face, taking note of where he might be able to dig deeper hand and footholds.

Back on the plateau, the clouds were darkening

and the air was thick and heavy. It was going to rain again.

He picked the helmet out of the pod, filled it with nuts and fronds from the rock safe, then hurried back to the cave. Holding the helmet in his teeth, he climbed up. As he swung his legs on to the ledge, the first fat raindrops started to fall, clapping and clicking through the leaves. He moved to the back of the cave where it was cool and dry and checked his welts. They were getting smaller and losing their redness. He felt okay, too, so he guessed the nuts were good to eat.

Outside, lightning flashed, thunder boomed and the rain poured down. But Valdez was cool and dry and feeding on orange nuts and sweet, blue fronds. "I have water," he said out loud. "I have food. I have shelter."

For the first time in three days, he felt pleased.

CHAPTER EIGHT

What was that? It was a grinding noise. Like the gnashing of small teeth.

Valdez opened his eyes with a start. He couldn't believe he'd fallen asleep again. It was dark, darker than on the plateau. Hardly any starlight or light from the moon penetrated the thick jungle canopy. He was just able to see simple outlines – the cave roof, the cave ledge – nothing more.

Had he been dreaming?

Was the noise part of a dream?

No. There it was again. Grinding, gnashing, slithering, coming from . . . the left.

Was the cave a home for another one of Eco's weird creatures? He didn't think so. The ledge was smooth and flat. He'd seen no debris or signs of animals. What was making the noise then?

Valdez sat very still. Something to the left.

Low down, sliding ever so slowly towards him. His breath caught in the back of his throat. His mouth went dry. He pulled his knees up under his chin. He saw it clearly.

Another creature.

Two bulbous, pitted sacs joined to a sloping head, scale-covered, four antennae. Luminous, bug-attracting teeth. Two long, multi-jointed legs with webbed, taloned feet. The creature slithered closer, grinding its teeth from side to side. Valdez knew he had to move. Quickly.

The tool. Get the knife open. He fumbled for it, got his hand to it, but couldn't open the blade. As he waved the useless tool in the air, the creature leaped. Valdez screamed, scrambled to his feet and threw the tool. It struck one of the sacs, bounced away, hit the shelter wall and sent sparks flying. Valdez grabbed it again, flicked the blade open and held it upward, but he didn't need it. The creature had backed off, slithered over the ledge and disappeared.

Valdez crept forward to make sure it was gone. It was then he noticed the pain in his thigh. He touched the spot and his fingers came away wet and sticky. It was blood. He had kept his eyes on the creature's head. He hadn't seen its flashing, taloned legs cut him. He pressed on the wound to stop the blood.

What was the creature? He guessed from its illuminated teeth that it was a night feeder. Maybe it had smelt him and come to investigate.

His heart beat fast.

I scared it away, he thought. Does that mean I'm brave? No. Anyone can be brave when there's no choice.

He sat down, keeping his hand pressed to the wound. Suddenly, the forest seemed alive with noises and movements. The darkness magnified everything, including his fear and uncertainty. What was going to happen to him? Would he be found? Was he going to die alone in the jungle . . . in this lonely, dangerous jungle? It didn't matter what he told himself, he knew he had been lucky. He'd only survived as long as this because of luck. And, sooner or later, that was going to run out.

He slipped deeper and deeper into a dark mood that finally brought tears – silent, terrified tears of despair that churned him up inside. They made him think he was useless. Hopeless. Yes, he'd gone to sleep feeling proud of himself, but the creature had reminded him that he was just a biologist who had lived indoors almost all of his life. He knew nothing about the wilderness. Nothing!

Then the tears were gone. His eyelids dropped and his head rolled to one side. There were moments of sleep, but at the same time he was alert. He heard all the small movements and noises in the forest. Then his mind did something strange. It was as if the tears had leaked out all his gloom. The time for feeling sorry for himself was over and he began planning, working out ways to protect the new shelter.

He would bring rocks up on to the ledge to make a barrier. He could have a fire, which would burn at night. No. He'd have to keep hauling up firewood and then he'd have to stay awake to refuel it. But a fire would be good. A fire would attract rescuers. Yes, but the steam and gas billowing from the plateau would attract them, too. And anyway how would he make a fire? His weary mind was a whirl of questions and suggestions. As he drifted into a deeper sleep, he somehow knew that he had changed.

The forest was quiet. Everything was becoming grey and slowly lightening up. Then, as the first shards of sunlight broke through the leaves, Valdez slowly woke up. Soon, he was painfully awake as the tiny hair-pullers attacked him again. He jerked his head up, slapping at the creatures that always seemed to find him. They buzzed away from his swinging hands – circling him, swooping in, spraying him, snatching a few loose, long hairs and shooting away, sending short, sharp pains through his head. He looked for the helmet. It was on the far side of the ledge. He crawled to it, jammed it on his head, then stood up.

Fully awake, he felt the pain in his thigh and looked down. The blood had hardened over the cut. He saw it was a shallow wound. The creature had probably only flung out a talon to protect itself. Valdez reminded himself once again that he was the new creature in this environment. He was the one who had to fit in. From now on, he told himself, when I come across a new creature, I will behave differently. I will be quiet, go about my business normally, not interfere with it and with luck it will do the same.

As he climbed down the cave wall and made

his way towards the nut and sweet frond trees, he remembered Umbro. He'd been so busy, he had hardly thought about him. At first, he'd hoped they'd find each other, but as time went on he knew that was less likely.

"If he is still alive," he said to himself, "then I will be rescued . . . He would have activated all emergency systems . . . I know he would have."

For his own sake, Valdez believed he would be rescued. And for Eco's sake, he believed Umbro was still alive. But he also knew that things didn't always go to plan. He pushed those thoughts away. Until he had facts, anything was still possible . . .

He shrugged. Nothing had changed. He hadn't been rescued and he was still lost, but he was determined he wouldn't give up. He was going to make sure he did everything he could to survive.

Then he realised that the forest had different lights. The light in the morning was different from the afternoon and evening. The morning light was brighter and clearer, with fewer shadows.

He saw a new plant for the first time. It had thick, pointed leaves and under the leaves were large, yellow and green striped bulging fruit. He knelt down and picked one. It was heavy and about the size of a small melon. He scratched off a sliver of skin and sniffed. A savoury smell – of tomato, cheese and bread. It was a savoury vegetable. He nibbled the sliver. Hard, dry and tasteless. That got him thinking some more.

Before Eco, the last time he had seen Sera was when he was a young boy. Over the years, along with most other humans, he had watched and listened to her weekly report on Eco's progress. His sister was familiar and famous, but Valdez realised that he didn't really know her. He had thought that would change once he got to Eco but it hadn't. He sighed. It had all turned out so wrong.

CHAPTER NINE

After collecting more nuts and sweet fronds, Valdez returned to the newly discovered plant. Although the nuts and fronds were tasty, they didn't fill him up for long. He needed food that would stop his gnawing hunger. He ripped one of the larger vegetables free and weighed it in his hand. It was probably full of goodness. But he couldn't eat it raw. When they'd been in the cloche, finding the edible food, someone had said that the fruits all tasted sweet and delicious while vegetables were often flavourless. Valdez was only half listening, but he was sure the instructor had said something about vegetables being tastier after cooking.

If he had a fire, he could wrap the vegetable in thick leaves and drop it into the smouldering ashes to cook slowly. His mouth began to water. He closed his eyes and could almost taste the bread, tomato and cheese. He shook his head. He didn't have any igniters or flares, so how was he going to cook the vegetable?

He carried the heavy vegetable to the curved rock on the plateau and placed it with the nuts and fronds in the rock safe. He stood with his hands on his hips and stared around. The plateau is volcanic, he thought. There's heat here. Steam. Hot water. If I can capture some of it, I can cook the vegetable.

Yes. A brilliant idea.

He had been around the edges of the plateau and swamp, but he hadn't explored it thoroughly. After eating a few more nuts and fronds, he set off along the forest fringe. The ground was like most of the plateau – bare, porous and craggy. But, as he moved inward towards the swamp, it changed slightly. There were ridges, crags and scars. In some places, he saw holes where rainwater had collected, but it was dirty and undrinkable.

When Valdez ran his hand through the pools, he found that they were all different temperatures. Was it hot water, or water heated by hot rocks? He wasn't sure, but he did know that, as he got closer to the swamp, the water got hotter.

Then, near one of the steam vents, right on the edge of the swamp, he found a large pool, about an arm's length across and deep. Big, wobbly bubbles rising to the steamy surface told him an underwater stream fed it. He dipped his finger in and yelped.

Scalding hot.

The pool was perfect. He grinned and hurried to the rock safe, grabbed the vegetable and carried it to the pool. Using the knife, he peeled away the stringy outer skin, then cut off a large chunk of meaty, savoury-smelling white flesh and held it above the hot pool's surface.

"Stop!" he shouted to himself. "Slow down."

The discovery of the vegetable and the hot pool to cook it in had excited him. It had made him rush. If he dropped the fleshy chunk into the pool, he wouldn't be able to get it out again.

He scratched his head, then sat on a flat rock to think things through. The chunk of vegetable had lost its delicious smell along with its freshness. It was turning brown and attracting tiny bugs. He threw it away. He needed to remember not to cut the vegetable until he was ready to cook. He scratched his head again then jumped to his feet.

Of course.

The hair-pullers.

Those tiny, annoying creatures were going to be very useful. Back in the forest he moved quietly through the undergrowth, ignoring the flitting movements of birds and flying bugs. But he was alert for larger movements and noises – the sorts of noises and movements he hadn't noticed until after the white, ape-like creature had got too close. He was learning, changing, adapting – using the forest to help himself.

It didn't take long to find the nests again. They hung on thick, floppy branches. Valdez walked around the base of the trees, looking for any fruit that might have dropped off, but there was none. He chose the tree that had the lowest nests, opened the knife and jumped up. One slash and a nest tumbled down. Jumping again and slashing another nest, he felt his boots sink and squelch into mud.

That was strange.

The ground around most of the trees was packed hard. He knelt down and saw a trickle of water flowing into his boot prints. When the prints filled up, the water flowed over the edge and under the tree. Valdez followed the flow. A few paces away, the trickle widened and quickened, then was joined by other small flows. The land was sloping downwards, too. Making sure he knew where the hair-pullers' nests were, he followed the running water.

Twenty or so paces down the slope, the water, now a stream as wide as his forearm, flowed over a bank and into a larger waterway that wound its way further downhill. The stream looked shallow and muddy, but there had to be eddies, pools, perhaps even waterfalls down there. And, if there was life in the forest, there was sure to be life in the stream.

More food.

He tucked that bit of information away in the back of his mind and scrambled back up the slope. He grabbed the hair-pullers' nests and headed back to the plateau.

It had rained again. The sun, well past midday, was heating the extra moisture, causing steam to build up across the plateau. Valdez dropped the nests beside the hot pool, then ate a couple of handfuls of nuts and fronds. That was all his stomach would take before it started to rumble and gurgle. He was desperate to eat something satisfying, something that would make him feel full. He hoped that would be the new vegetable.

He pulled his coveralls down to his waist and noticed the red welts had all but disappeared. Then he looked carefully at the nests, at the clever way the hair-pullers had woven them, tangling bits of reeds, leaves, tiny soft branches and even his hair into perfectly formed baskets. He was sure they would hold a small chunk of vegetable flesh in the hot water without breaking up. All he had to do was attach a cord to the top of them so they could be lowered and raised.

Valdez cut three long reed leaves from a plant at the edge of the swamp. After stripping away the hard, fibrous spines, he split the leaves into thin cords. He criss-crossed two cords together, then threaded them around the top of each nest, tied a knot and pulled it tight. It held easily.

He collected another vegetable, skinned it, cut out two chunks of flesh and placed them in the small baskets. He was dangling them over the hot pool when he stopped and slumped back on the rocks. He couldn't cook the food until he'd tested the water. He was a scientist. It should have been the first thing he did. The yellow, brown and black stains around the pool showed there were minerals in the water. Was the water poisonous? He couldn't be totally sure, but he could taste-test it. Better still, he could get the insects to test it – the insects he'd found in the water hollows of the large-leaved trees.

He dropped the baskets and ran back to the cave to get the helmet. He ripped out the padding, earpieces and radio receiver, then scooped up some water from the pool and took it to the water trees. He waited for the pool water to cool, then flicked as many insects as he could into the helmet. They seemed to carry on swimming freely, so he returned to the plateau.

Valdez sat in the curved rock and shook his head a little – not because he was annoyed, but because he was surprised. All day he'd been faced with problems. They were small problems, nowhere near as complicated as Eco's, but, as he solved each one, he knew he was improving his chances of staying alive, which meant they were just as important.

He collected another vegetable, chewed a few more nuts and fronds, then looked at the insects in the helmet again. They were still swimming about, so he dipped his finger in and tasted the water. Nothing odd. He flicked out the insects, scooped up a cupped handful and sucked and slurped it. It tasted a bit metallic, but nothing sharp, burning or bitter.

He waited a few more minutes, then scooped up and tasted another handful. It was a rough test, but he was fairly sure the water was okay.

Once more, he took a fresh vegetable to the hot pool, stripped it and cut out two chunks. He placed the chunks into the baskets, then lowered them into the pool. The water bubbled and sizzled around them. Almost immediately Valdez pulled the baskets out again. Seeing the pieces of vegetable were still lodged inside the baskets, he lowered them again, then sat down to wait.

He wasn't sure how long the vegetable chunks would take to cook, so every now and then he raised the baskets and checked them by poking them with the knife. When the chunks were bright yellow and soft right through, he turned them out of the baskets on to large green leaves and cut them into small pieces. They looked yellow, bland, dry – a bit like a sweet potato – but

Valdez didn't think he had ever seen something so delicious. He got down and sniffed the hot steam and caught a whiff of hot bread and tomatoes. He wanted to gobble them up straight away.

Slowly, ever so slowly, the vegetable cooled and Valdez was able to pick up a piece and hold it without scalding his fingers. He bit into it and groaned. It had no taste. Nothing. Just a dry, floury lump. He chewed the lump, then swallowed, and only then was he hit by an explosion of taste – the warmest, doughiest bread, the sweetest tomato and the tangiest cheese, all rolled into one flavour burst. He groaned again, but this time it was with pleasure.

Without thinking, he grabbed the rest of the cooked pieces, stuffed them into his mouth, and chewed and swallowed. Once again he was hit by the intense taste. The cooked vegetable was glorious. He was sure it was the best food he had ever tasted. It sat heavily in his stomach, but he still wanted more.

He stood up to collect another vegetable. It was wasteful to cook just a few chunks at a time. He decided to cook the entire fresh vegetable and store the cooked chunks in the rock safe with the nuts and fronds. Later, he would move the food store up to the cave.

Suddenly, his stomach turned upside down and he was hit with crippling cramps – cramps that bent him over and squeezed the breath out of him. He dropped to his knees and his stomach erupted. Bent down on all fours, he vomited, throwing up all the vegetable, nuts and fronds. He retched again and again, his stomach convulsing until it ached so hard he was sure it had ripped apart.

The cave.

He wanted to get to the cave – get to shelter and lie down. He crawled a few paces then curled into a tight ball, jammed his eyes shut and cried out. His long, lonely wail echoed through the forest.

CHAPTER TEN

He had no fever, so he was quite sure he hadn't been poisoned. If it wasn't the water and it wasn't the vegetable, then he'd just eaten too fast again. When would he learn that he couldn't just force something unfamiliar on his system? He had to eat slowly, and he had to eat small amounts.

He was at the cooking pool again. All morning he had sat in the hollow rock, waiting for his stomach to settle. Some time after midday, he stood up and wandered weakly into the forest to drink from the cup leaves. He took small sips and the water stayed down. Then he nibbled a sweet frond and ate a few nuts. They stayed down, too. His stomach still ached, but that was probably from the retching and hunger. He was learning, painfully, that everything in the wild takes time. If he tried to rush things, he was going to be hurt.

He collected and cut up another vegetable, then put the pieces in the baskets and lowered them into the pool. After the pieces were cooked, he cut them again and, once they were cool, ate them, drinking plenty of water between mouthfuls. The taste was just as delicious and everything stayed down, but he only ate a small amount. Eat a little and often, he reminded himself. Little and often.

It wasn't enough. Whatever he ate never filled him up. As soon as he had finished swallowing, his stomach craved more. Or was it craving different food? He thought about what he had been eating – sweet fronds, salty nuts and tasty vegetables. Were they all from the same food group? The fronds and vegetables were, but the nuts had to be different. After he'd eaten them, he always felt a little fuller. Did he need to eat more nuts?

Perhaps.

Then he remembered the stream and the food that might be there. He grabbed the baskets and made his way to the trickling stream, following it down the bank to where the forest became thicker. At the bottom of the bank, he cut some branches and spread them around so he wouldn't lose his way when he returned.

A few paces on, he saw that all the small streams had formed into a larger stream. He followed this further downhill and almost fell into a wide volcanic pool, with edges that crumbled into fine, powdery sand.

Valdez peered into the pool. He had no idea how deep it was. He found a long, broken branch in the forest and cut off the dead branches and leaves. When he stood it up straight, it was almost double his height. He thrust it down into the water. It disappeared below the surface, then bobbed back up and floated away to one side. But Valdez wasn't watching the stick. He was watching the water. When he'd put the stick into the water, he'd seen silver flashes darting in all directions, and a darker, longer shape snaking below them.

Fish.

He wasn't interested in the tiny sprats. It was the large fish that he wanted. And, as he stared into the dark pool, a new certainty formed in his mind. He would catch it. Yes. That would be his task for day four – a task to keep his mind off his hopes of rescue.

The thought was always there, lurking at the back of his mind. Whenever it distracted him, he repeated the survival instructor's words: "Identify everything that may be useful. Ignore anything you have no control over."

He was back by the broken branches at the bottom of the bank when he heard it. It was a sound he'd never heard in the forest before, but it was a sound he knew – the slow, throbbing whoosh of a shuttle. He stood frozen, straining to listen. It had to be the rescue shuttle. The throbbing whoosh came and went as the shuttle climbed and dived, climbed and dived.

Searching.

Searching for him.

Valdez scrambled up the bank. But it was harder going up than coming down. His boots wouldn't grip. The more he tried to bury his toes into the soft, wet ground, the more they gouged out mud and carried him back to the bottom. Valdez ran out of breath. He stopped, then moved along the bank to where there was undisturbed earth. He thrust the knife into the ground above him, then planted his feet carefully and pulled himself up. Up, up, he went, ever so slowly. Then he was over the top and running through the forest, waving his arms and shouting wildly.

"I'm down here! You found me!"

Thoughts raced through his mind. Had they found Umbro? Did he lead them here? Or was the shuttle on a routine grid search? He didn't care. All the hope that had been trapped deep in the back of his mind was out. It rushed into his waving arms, his pumping legs and his screaming voice. Who was in the shuttle? Was it Sera or another pilot? Again, he didn't care. They were here and that was all that mattered.

Valdez burst out of the forest, on to the plateau. He looked up. Nothing. But the sound was still there. He swivelled his head, tracking the noise.

Coming closer?

No.

Moving away.

Slowly, the throbbing whoosh got fainter and fainter. Valdez wished, willed the shuttle to turn back, but it didn't. It was gone.

The shuttle had to be working a grid pattern. It would have tracking sensors, but none of them would have sensed the Venom shuttle because it was buried in the swamp, and none of them would have sensed Valdez because, deep in the forest, he could easily have been a woodland animal like the white ape. Once the shuttle had completed its grid, this part of the rainforest would be crossed off and it would move somewhere else, unlikely to return.

Valdez stood still. Big, wet tears rolled down his cheeks. Then the sky darkened, lightning lit up the rocks and trees and great claps of thunder boomed all around. Valdez didn't move. He stayed in the warm, wet rain and cried until he couldn't cry any more. He couldn't go on. Not without the belief that he would be rescued. It had been so close, but now the shuttle was gone, taking his belief with it.

The rain eased and he turned and walked through the forest to the cave. Soaked through, he climbed on to the ledge and sat down. It was then he noticed he still had the knife in his hand. He flung it angrily behind him. He didn't see it bounce and spark off the rock wall. He didn't see a part of the handle break off and fly away. He lay down with his eyes open and stared at the ceiling. He didn't feel thirsty. He didn't feel hungry. He didn't feel anything.

CHAPTER ELEVEN

After collecting clumps of moss, needles and leaves for bedding, Valdez stayed in the shelter the rest of the day. Late in the afternoon, he drifted off a few times but, as darkness settled in, he sat up, stretched his arms and sighed. He knew he couldn't give up. He had to keep believing that he would be rescued because, if he didn't believe it would happen, then it probably wouldn't. Belief was everything.

Okay. So a search shuttle had passed over him. But, after four days, they were still searching. That was good. He knew Sera wouldn't give up. When the grid pattern process was unsuccessful, she would use more detailed methods. They would find him . . . eventually . . . so he had to keep going. He had to survive.

He found a few nuts and sweet fronds in

his pockets and ate them then looked up at the darkening sky. There was still enough light to go down to the pool to cook some more vegetable. He sighed again. He couldn't be bothered. Nibbling on the last of the fronds, he thought back over the time since the crash.

Each day there had been a problem. He had had to find food, water and shelter. They were anxious days and the tasks had taken time. They had distracted him, stopped him from thinking about his treacherous situation.

He needed another task. What had he been doing when he heard the shuttle?

The stream pool.

Yes.

There were many small fish and at least one large one. Or was it an eel? "I've got to catch it," he said to himself. "Catch it and eat it."

Boiled in water, a fish or eel would be much tastier than nuts, fronds or the vegetable. His stomach rumbled again. The pains were back. Great, gnawing, aching pains. He picked at the crumbs on his coveralls just as the last of the light left the forest and the hair-pullers swooped on him. His helmet was on the plateau. Dancing and yelping, he tried to swat them away, but it was no good. Then it was dark and they were gone, but not without large chunks of his hair.

He settled back on his bedding. Curled up to stop the aches in his stomach, he decided to work out some way to catch the fish. He would need his knife. He patted his pockets but it wasn't there.

Then he remembered that he had thrown it against the shelter wall.

Where had it fallen?

On his hands and knees, he searched the cave floor. He found it right on the corner of the ledge. One bounce further and it would have fallen into the bushes below. He grabbed it, annoyed with himself. "The knife is important," he said out loud. "Look after it."

A sound stopped him as he moved towards his bedding. At times during the day, the screechy shrillness of birds, animals and insects could be deafening, but at night the small, unusual, unfamiliar sounds seemed almost as loud.

Valdez listened. Was it the beast that had crept into the cave before? He flicked the knife open. The sound . . . was it friendly or dangerous?

He dropped to his stomach and wriggled to

the ledge. Whatever it was seemed to be moving away on the forest floor, shuffling, slithering.

A snake? No, heavier than a snake. And not slithering but dragging, rustling the leaf litter and breaking twigs.

Valdez tightened his grip on the knife and concentrated. Yes. The sound was getting fainter. Then it stopped altogether. His muscles tensed as he heard a cough, a rush of air, then the dragging starting again. The creature stopped four more times before it faded completely from earshot. He waited until he was sure it was long gone, then he crawled back to his bedding. He fell into a fitful sleep, waking often to listen to the forest sounds.

Valdez woke early, just as light began filtering through the trees. When he sat up he found the open knife still in his hand. Part of its ceramic handle had broken away when it hit the cave wall. He shut the blade and saw something glimmering on the knife's handle. Walking to the ledge, he held it up to the light. There was a small, clear cylinder fixed into the handle. When he shook the knife, an amber liquid moved through the cylinder.

What was it?

He turned the knife over and searched for a hidden clip that might release the cylinder. There wasn't one. He knocked the handle hard, but the cylinder wouldn't budge. It seemed the only way to get it out was to smash it. He didn't want to do that until he knew what it was. It could be anything – medicine, a catalyst, an enzyme – or perhaps nothing, just a useless ornament. Besides, it was day five. He had things to do. He dropped the knife into his pocket and clambered down the rock face.

Sunlight was leaking over the treetops as he reached the plateau. He grabbed his helmet, tipped out the collected water and jammed it on to his head. The hair-pullers quickly appeared and Valdez laughed as they buzzed and clicked and tried to spray him. Frustrated, they disappeared into the swamp in search of easier prey.

It was then that he remembered the creature in the night and headed back towards the cave. As he got close, he slowed down, stopping to brush away leaves and branches, searching for tracks. About five paces from the cave entrance, he found them.

Crawling beneath thick, yellow-leaved trees

and bushes, he followed the tracks. Suddenly, he jumped up. At the base of a spindly tree he saw a small brown mound. In fact, it was more of a lump – an irregular shape covered in masses of nodules. Perhaps it was the creature's droppings. Valdez went a little closer and sniffed.

Nothing.

Was it alive?

Valdez picked up a branch. Holding an arm in front of his eyes to fend off any squirting liquid, he poked the lump. It immediately split down the middle and opened up. Inside was a pile of perfectly shaped, small blue balls.

Eggs?

He poked one. It felt soft and rubbery. Something in his brain suggested food.

Using the stick, he dragged it towards him. Keeping an eye on the open mound, he picked the ball up. It was soft to touch. He wiped dirt from one side and sniffed it. He rolled it between his fingers. He took out the knife and cut it. An orange, oily substance ran through his fingers. It was an egg. He sniffed the yolk. No smell again. He wondered what they'd taste like cooked.

CHAPTER TWELVE

Valdez had eaten eggs – tasteless powdered eggs – at Home Base. He didn't like them. They were rubbery and dry and stuck to the roof of his mouth.

These eggs looked different. He would put them in a cooking basket and boil them. The nuts and fronds would have to wait just as the fish lurking at the bottom of the stream pool could wait. He had new food.

He set off to collect a basket. As he walked, the hunger hit him again, stronger than ever. After five days, his body was demanding more than just fronds, nuts and vegetables.

He slid down the muddy bank and grabbed the basket. On his way back to the plateau, he had a sudden thought. Again, he hadn't considered all possibilities. What if the mound could move? It didn't look as if it could, but how did he know for sure?

He groaned.

He should have taken the rest of the eggs out of the mound when he found them. Once again, he hadn't planned ahead.

He pushed his way through the forest, running as fast as he could. Collapsing on the ground beneath the yellow-leaved trees, he brushed away the leaf litter and let out a gasp of relief. The mound was still there.

Valdez felt dizzy. He stayed low for a moment, until he had his breath back and his head had cleared. Then he dragged the eggs free of their nest and put them carefully into his coveralls pockets.

Back at the cooking pool, he laid his treasure out on the rocks. Fifteen rich blue eggs.

He put one into the basket and dropped it into the pool. The water fizzed and bubbled. He counted to thirty, then lifted the basket. The egg looked darker and was still soft to touch. He lowered it into the pool again and counted another thirty. This time the egg's skin was firm and had turned black. Valdez grabbed it. Too hot. He dropped it. It bounced then split on the rocks.

Bright red yolk seeped into the cracks.

Valdez was stunned. He felt tears welling in his eyes. How could he have been so stupid! It was only an egg, but it was precious food – food that couldn't be wasted.

He dipped a finger in the yolk and licked it. The taste was good – a biscuity, smoky flavour. It set off the grumbling in his stomach again.

Quickly, he put two more eggs into the basket and lowered them into the pool. After counting to sixty, he rolled the black balls on to green leaves and waited for them to cool. It seemed to take forever.

Finally, he picked one up and bit into it. The outer skin gave way easily and the soft centre ran into his mouth, filling it with the smoky flavours he had tasted before.

Delicious.

He pushed the rest of the egg into his mouth, then quickly ate the other one, too. His stomach, enjoying the rich, new food, screamed for more. He was tempted, but he knew he had to eat slowly – little and often. And he wanted them to last.

He smiled.

He was planning ahead. His hunger was still

there, but it had dulled to an ache. He could deal with that.

He looked at the remaining twelve blue eggs on the rocks. They were the most valuable things he had ever owned. Carefully, he gathered them up, carried them up to the cave and covered them with rocks.

He'd decided to eat two a day. The eggs would last six days. The rescuers would be back by then.

His belief was stronger than ever.

CHAPTER THIRTEEN

Valdez had been excited about arriving on Eco, but his welcome had been disappointing. Sera had met him at the docking station. She'd shaken his hand and hugged him stiffly without smiling, mumbling, "Great to see you." Then her buttonpager had beeped and she'd left him with Umbro.

In the weeks that followed it had been Umbro who'd helped him settle in – organised his accommodation, taken him on a tour of Home Base and set up his work routine.

He'd seen and spoken to Sera perhaps twice a week, and then only for a few minutes. She had asked him how he was getting on, but hadn't really listened to his answers. She was totally distracted. With the approaching arrival of the immigrants, Valdez knew she was anxious to have everything perfect at Home Base, but so was everyone else.

No. Her constant frown, gruffness and all-round unhappiness must have been signs of deeper worries.

Three days passed and, on each day, Valdez set himself the same routine.

He woke early, got up and repacked the moss, needles and leaves in his bedding. Then he climbed down into the forest, drank a few handfuls of water and set off to collect his daily supply of nuts and fronds.

The fronds seemed to grow only in one area and he knew he wasn't the only creature eating them. The birds found them delicious, too. The fruiting season for the sweet fronds seemed to be almost over and they were becoming more scarce, but luckily there was an endless supply of nuts.

After he had gathered his harvest, he returned to the plateau and boiled up chunks of the fleshy vegetable. When he'd first eaten it, the taste had been exquisite, but now, after having it three times a day, he was already sick of it. After the vegetable, he ate an egg. It seemed to give him more energy and helped to deaden his hunger.

During the days, he'd been busy. The cave was looking less like a cave and more like a hut. He had thrown out the crunchy leaves and needles he'd used for bedding and made a new bed. He'd cut two long branches and two shorter branches, fixed them into a rectangle, tied the ends with reeds, then packed armfuls of soft, dry leaf litter and mounds of moss into the space. To stop any leaves and dry needles from scratching him, he lay large, fleshy green leaves on top.

He kept a supply of nuts and fronds in a new rock safe. He put the eggs in there as well, wrapped in a couple of hair-pullers' nests.

Valdez had tracked the egg-laying creature, but hadn't found any other mounds, so his thoughts had returned to the fish in the stream pool and how to catch it.

Spearing was too difficult. He thought about a net, but that meant undoing many hair-pullers' nests, then weaving them into a larger net. That would take too long. The best idea was a stick and line. There were plenty of long, thin branches he could use. And he was sure he could make a line from cutting and stripping fibres from the swamp reeds. The problem was a hook.

The pick in the multi-tool was the right length and it had a sharp point, too, but when he tried to bend it between two rocks it snapped in half. He had to find something else.

He searched the plateau and cave and the area between the cave and the frond trees. He stripped bits off the pod, but they were too thin, too flimsy or too tough. There was nothing.

But he didn't give up. It was good to have another problem to solve. It helped fill the day and stopped him thinking about the rescue. Since the shuttle fly-over, he had tried not to think about it. And if he did, then he immediately began a job – collecting more food, clearing the track between the cave and the plateau or collecting more bedding.

He had other food-catching ideas, too. A fall trap seemed like a good one. He could set out fresh nuts, fronds or even a bit of cooked vegetable. Some heavy rocks would be balanced above the food. When an animal ate the food, it would set off a trigger that released the rocks to crash on to the animal and stun or kill it. But Valdez hadn't worked out what to use for a trigger.

Another idea was to weave a couple of

hairpullers' nests into a small net. The net, with bits of vegetable or nuts inside, would be fixed to a long pole and lifted into the treetops. When a bird hopped inside the net to get the food, Valdez would yank both the net and the bird to the ground.

Both ideas needed more thought. But, for the time being, he'd decided to work on the fish hook. Fishing was the simplest way to get more food. If only he could find something to use as a hook.

He found it in the most obvious place.

It was day eight. He was at the cooking hole, boiling vegetable, when one of the chunks rolled out of a hole in the cooking basket. Over time, the hot water had been slowly unravelling the hair-pullers' weaving.

Valdez grabbed a long-handled stick that had a naturally formed loop on one end, worked it under the floating vegetable chunk and brought it to the surface. As he tipped the vegetable on to a green leaf, he saw that he'd caught something else in the loop. A small bone. Valdez stared at it, then suddenly whooped. He pulled up the cooking basket, waited for the water to clear, then thrust the looped stick back into the pool and hauled up a shiny white skeleton.

Bones.

Valdez whooped again. He was sure he could make an excellent fish hook from these bones.

CHAPTER FOURTEEN

It didn't take long.

Valdez had already selected his pole – a long, cylinder-like stick. He'd rubbed the bark smooth with some sandpapery leaves he'd found close to the cave. One end of the stick fitted neatly into his palm. The other end stretched to a fine tip where there were nodules on which to tie a length of reed fibre. The fibre was as thin as cotton, but many times stronger. For length, Valdez had plaited three strips of fibre together, end to end. He figured they'd be long enough to reach the bottom of the pool.

With the pole complete, he went to work on the hook. The bones had probably belonged to some animal that had stumbled into the pool in the dark. He guessed its fur and meat had been boiled away, leaving a clean, white skeleton.

Valdez ran his fingers along the backbone until he came to the thickest part, which was about the width of his thumb. He set the bone on a flat rock, opened the knife and sawed off a piece about the length of his small finger. Now came the delicate work. He scratched out the shape he wanted with the knife. Then, digging the knife point in along the scratches, he gouged out a bent, barbed hook. It was slow, painstaking work.

Valdez worked on the hook all day, using rocks to grind down the bone to make smooth, sharp edges. Then, as the sun started to dip behind the trees, he decided he was finished.

He had a hook to catch a fish.

It was such a small thing. He stared at it and shook his head. At Home Base, he would have designed it on a computer, then sent the design instructions to a machine that could tool a perfect hook in two minutes. That was okay, but seeing and holding something that he'd made with his own hands seemed worth all the time and effort.

There wasn't enough light left to make the trip to the pool, but first thing the next morning he would be there. He licked his lips. Cooked fish for breakfast. What a thought.

He gathered his bits together, then boiled up some more vegetable, plus extra for bait. He wasn't sure whether the fish would be attracted to the fronds, nuts or boiled vegetable. He'd try them all, starting with the boiled vegetable because it was easily kneaded on to the hook.

Valdez slept well that night and even dreamed of catching a huge, silvery fish – one that leaped and jumped about the pool so madly it snapped his hook, his line and his pole.

He woke before the sun was up and drank some water, then gathered a good number of nuts and fronds. After eating a few, along with an egg, he collected his fishing pole and set off for the pool.

It was just light when he reached it. He set the pole down and looked around. The pool was about thirty paces across and fed by a network of small streams, all flowing off the higher slopes. Across the pool, the water flowed over some low rocks and fell down into another, larger stream. One to explore later.

He stared at the pool's mirror surface, trying to work out where to throw his line. The fish was probably in the deepest part, which, judging by the darkness of the water, appeared to be right in front of him. Nothing seemed to be moving down there, so he picked up a rock and flicked it into the water, then immediately regretted it. He wanted to catch the fish, not scare it.

He unwrapped the lump of boiled vegetable and spat on it to add moisture, then kneaded it into a squashy mass. He sat there, absorbed in the task, so fixed on catching the fish that he missed all the warning signs. They came one after another.

He held the pole, bent the tip and tugged on the thread. A sharp squawk sounded above him. He didn't hear it. He tested the hook knot, then moulded a piece of vegetable on to the barb.

The forest had gone silent. He didn't notice. He took another piece of doughy vegetable, crumbled it in his fingers and flicked them into the pool. The fragments hit the water like tiny raindrops.

A shadow fell across him. He didn't see it.

Suddenly, the pool was a splashing frenzy as the big fish thrashed about, gobbling the bait.

The squawk sounded again and the shadow lengthened. But it was too late.

Valdez heard a whoosh of air and at last he

looked up. He saw a bird. No, an eel.

An eelbird!

He saw a flash of its long, twisting body with shimmering purple skin, pumping pink wings, long, wrinkly, taloned claws, needle-sharp teeth and a viper tongue in the split second before the eelbird hit him and flung him into the pool. He sank. He thrashed about, trying to get to the surface, but the eelbird sat above him. Is this it? he thought. Is this where I die?

No!

He thrashed some more, broke the surface and took a breath. Then the eelbird hit him again, pushing him back under. His head hit the rock wall and he felt a stinging pain in his leg. Again, he flung his arms and legs around and burst to the surface. The eelbird was gone.

Valdez swam to the edge of the pool and hung there, gasping and sucking air. Then, slowly, he lifted his head and saw the eelbird in the tree above him. Its feathers flickered and flashed in the sunlight. Blood from the grazes on his forehead ran into his eyes. He wiped it away with his sleeve, then pulled himself out of the pool.

Once more, he heard the whoosh of wings.

The eelbird hit him front on, smashing him back into the pool. Valdez's head spun. He saw bright lights before his eyes. Spluttering and coughing, he fought his way to the surface.

The eelbird swooped down again, raking its talons across the water. Valdez dived and felt the claws grab at his coveralls. He dived deeper and swam to the far side of the pool before surfacing beside the outflow. Staying low in the water, he looked for the eelbird. It was back on its perch, watching him.

Why had the eelbird attacked? Valdez was still convinced that Eco animals were not naturally aggressive. Surely they couldn't all have mutation problems. No. It was something else. Perhaps the bird was protecting something. Babies? Eggs?

Valdez didn't know. But he did know he had to get out of the pool and away from the eelbird.

Moving slowly, he crawled up on to the rocks and waited. The eelbird didn't move. They sat on opposite sides of the pool, watching each other. Then, suddenly, Valdez rolled over, scrambled to his feet and dived into the nearest undergrowth. He could hear the eelbird whooshing, swooping and squawking, but he didn't stop.

Slithering, sliding and skidding, he clambered up the bank. Gasping, he stopped under a tall tree with low branches and looked back towards the pool. The eelbird hadn't followed him. It was hopping about on the rocks. It stopped beside his fishing pole then leaned down, pecked the dough off the hook and flicked it into the pool.

The pool surface bubbled and boiled. Even from a distance, Valdez could see the shimmering purple skins and flashing pink fins of baby eelbirds. He shook all over. If he hadn't escaped from the pool, he would surely have been their dinner.

Valdez dragged himself back to the cave and shrugged out of the wet coveralls. The bleeding on his forehead had stopped. He checked his leg and saw a long, shallow gash across his calf. He lay down on his bed and closed his eyes, his heart still beating fast. Although his body cried out for rest, he didn't want to sleep. Not until he had made some sense of the attack.

The eelbird had to be amphibious. Its young were in the pool. Perhaps they were ready to morph into birds? Once again, he had wandered into another animal's domain. He had disturbed the balance and the animal had attacked. All it was doing was protecting its young. He was the blunderer and it had almost cost him his life.

Valdez wasn't angry or scared. He was annoyed that he'd missed the warning signals. Once again the forest had taught him an important lesson. The forest was a dangerous place for all living things. The key to survival was to be sharp-eyed and wary – always. He had to survive.

The rescuers were coming.

CHAPTER FIFTEEN

After the announcement of the virus had been made at the meeting in the Great Hall, everything on Eco had changed. Apart from one or two virus observation flights to the different habitats, everyone had been restricted to Home Base. All personnel had been assigned tasks to assist the development of the antidote. Everyone knew that the immigrants and their own existence on Eco depended on it. Sera had become even more grim as she struggled to oversee everything. Then, after she fell out with Umbro, he had changed, too.

Valdez had been helping him analyse some of the antidote trial results. When he was absorbed in his work, Umbro often talked to himself. He was speaking his thoughts out loud and, as the trials went on, he had talked more and more about Sera. Valdez had heard every word and, the more he heard, the more he became convinced that she was as big a problem as the virus.

Valdez stayed in the cave for the rest of the day. Between sleeps, he put clumps of cool, wet leaves on the gash on his leg. He ate a few nuts and fronds, but he wasn't very hungry.

Probably delayed shock, he thought.

But he knew his hunger would return, stronger than ever, and he still had the problem of finding food. He couldn't go back to the pool, but there might be something in the larger stream he'd seen below the pool.

Yes, he'd search there. As long as he stayed alert, he'd be okay. He knew he would still make mistakes, but hopefully they would be small ones, not life-threatening like the one he'd made that morning. Now that he'd had time to think carefully about what happened, it did scare him. It wasn't the actual attack, because he could have avoided that, but he was scared of being seriously injured. The eelbird could have torn strips of skin from his body or held him under the water for longer. He could have drowned.

Dead.

Well, dead was dead. Nothing could be done about that.

No. An injury, like a broken leg or arm, was the real danger. A broken limb would be agony. It would stop him moving about. At the moment, he was able to keep busy – searching for new food and improving his living areas. But, if he couldn't move about, collect his nuts and fronds and cook the vegetable, then he would surely die. He had to stay fit. He had to stay healthy. Valdez stuck another cold compress of mashed-up leaves on his cut. With luck, they'd keep out the dirt and any infection.

Sometime late in the afternoon he drifted off. When he woke up, it was dark. Something had disturbed him. He lay still and opened his eyes slowly, blinking, adjusting to the dimness. Moving only his eyes, he looked around. He was on his side. He could see the cave opening and he could hear scuffling. It was coming from behind him.

There was something in the cave.

Every muscle and nerve in Valdez's body wanted him to scream, jump up and run out of the cave, but he held himself rigid. Slowly, ever so slowly, he turned his head. The leaves beneath him scrunched. He smelt a musky, animal odour.

There was an animal in the cave.

Again, he stopped himself from making any sudden movements. He heard the scuffling again, then something burning – a burning stink of hair or fabric. He stretched his neck and saw the animal. It was at the back of the cave, sniffing and pawing the rock food safe.

The animal was the size of a small bear. It had dark red fur, two powerful hind legs, a bushy tail and yellow spines along its back. Each time it moved, a flash of sparks leaped off its spines and scorched its fur.

The bear knocked the rocks away from the food, scattering the nuts and fronds, and grabbed the eggs. Then, one by one, it ate them. When it was finished, it turned and shuffled towards the cave entrance. It moved past Valdez, its rippling and sparking body giving the cave an eerie glow. Valdez watched it go. Somehow he knew it wasn't going to hurt him. Soon the bear had climbed over the ledge and darkness filled the cave again.

Valdez rolled on to his back and let out a long, slow breath. He'd done it. He'd wanted to scream, jump and run. He'd even wanted to hit the bear with the stick that lay next to his bed, but he hadn't. He had stayed calm, and the bear had left him alone. It was only interested in the eggs.

Valdez had been right. The Eco animals were not aggressive, they were defensive. If someone or something invaded their territory to threaten their homes or family, then they defended – strongly. Just like the eelbird. In the forest, Valdez had come to learn that there was some instinctive understanding between the animals. They gave off some sort of signal that said, "Leave me alone and I'll leave you alone." It was the natural way.

The encounter with the bear creature was important for Valdez. If he had acted differently, he was sure he would have been injured – perhaps too injured to look after himself. He closed his eyes, feeling pleased with himself. Then he remembered that all the eggs were gone and he realised what that meant.

CHAPTER SIXTEEN

After the Great Hall meeting, Umbro had spent part of each day scanning his console. Valdez had sat behind him in front of his own console. Every now and then, Umbro had called to him to refresh, highlight, update, delete or add in new antidote trial data. Being so close to him, Valdez couldn't ignore his other mutterings.

"It's not going to work . . . outdated practice . . . flawed processes . . . I have the antidote formula . . . Why won't she give me the master computer's input code to trial it? . . . She won't even discuss it . . . I told her I won't take the credit . . . I'll say she developed the formula . . . I know Eco is her special project . . . But she has to listen to me . . . I have the key to Eco's future . . . Blind pride . . . Self-important arrogance . . . There will be a disaster and she will pay . . ."

When he first heard the grumblings, Valdez had wanted to defend his sister, but the more Umbro muttered, and the more he saw the two of them together, the more certain he became that Umbro was right.

The days had become blurred, one rolling into another. How long had he been lost? Ten days? Perhaps more? He'd stopped counting. Counting the days only reminded him of how long it had been since he had seen another human. It was better just to wake up and get on with things.

He still believed he would be rescued. He was important, and Umbro was even more important. He was the only one who could save Eco. Sera and the Security Council would do everything they could to find them.

He'd stopped thinking about Sera. Her betrayal no longer seemed important. The only thing that was important was food. The nut and frond trees were almost bare, but he had stumbled across another discovery.

He'd been beside the frond tree when suddenly the forest around him erupted with squawks, screeches, barks and squeals. Before, Valdez would have charged back to the safety of the plateau. Now he froze, listened, looked around and even sniffed the air.

The clamour died away, then immediately rose up again. This time it was further away. Valdez figured it was about a hundred paces to the left. Slowly and quietly, he walked towards it, avoiding dry leaves and twigs. As he got closer, he moved into thinner bushes for a better view. In front of him he could see four large, low-growing bushes with small, oval leaves and thick clusters of red berries. Many monkeys – small, with grey fur, yellow-ringed tails and bright black eyes – were leaping about the bushes, feeding on the ripe berries. Their hands and fingers were stained red. Valdez watched them for a few moments, chose a long-trunked tree as a landmark, then moved quietly back to the frond trees. When the monkeys had gone, he would return to gather some berries.

His diet was unvarying – nuts, fronds, lots of boiled vegetable and now fresh, ripe berries. He picked only enough for each day. He had also returned the rock food safe to the plateau. He didn't want any more night visitors.

The extra food helped to fill him up but, as always, only for a short time. Desperate to find something more satisfying, he had explored the stream below the eelbird pool. He'd wandered along its banks for at least five hundred paces, stopping often to sit and stare into the depths, hoping to see something. He figured there had to be stream life other than the eelbirds.

His patience finally paid off.

Further downstream, he found some deep, fast-flowing water and among the small rapids he saw flashes of red. He watched the flickering red spots moving up and down the stream bed. He figured that, if they were moving against the current, then they had to be fish or shellfish. Valdez felt his heart quicken, but he didn't move. He stood still, working out a plan. This time he was determined not to fail.

He collected and untangled more hair-pullers' nests, then retied them with reed fibres to make one big basket about the size of four hand spans. He tied another long thread to one end of the basket so he could lower it into the deep water. He tested all the knots and made sure the opening was big enough for a decent-sized fish to get in.

He boiled up some vegetable for bait. Then he set off.

Today was fish day.

Valdez moved quietly past the stream pool and paused on the far side. The eelbird was keeping watch on its perch. He shivered. It couldn't have been on its perch the first time he went to the pool, otherwise it would have attacked him when he thrust the long stick into the water.

He moved on, following the pool water down a steep bank and along a rutted track. The stream deepened, wound its way around large trees and rocks, then flowed into a shallow pool. Valdez walked past the pool and sat on the bank. Below his feet, the red spots moved about in the fast water. He sat still. He looked up into the trees. He scanned the nearby forest. He turned his head into the light breeze and sniffed.

When he was sure he was alone, he opened the parcel of boiled vegetable, broke it into chunks and stuffed it into the basket. Slowly, he lowered the basket into the water. The current tugged it. Valdez let out more thread and the basket settled beside the bank. He didn't have to wait long. Just a few minutes later, he felt a heavy weight on the thread, then several sharp tugs. Something was in the basket and struggling to get out. Jumping to his feet, he hauled in the thread and dragged the basket to the surface. He grinned when he saw flashes of red through the gaps in the weave. He pulled the basket on to the bank. It jumped about and he could hear snapping and clacking. He stretched the opening and two long antennae poked out, followed by three large, snapping claws. Valdez shut the opening.

He had caught a freshwater lobster.

He grinned. He'd been so quiet. He'd been so careful. He'd been so controlled and so alert, but he couldn't keep it up any longer. He leaped up and down. He threw his arms in the air and shouted, "Lobster! I have a lobster to eat! Delicious lobster!"

And the whole forest seemed to reply with a rush of wings, a cackle of caws, rustling undergrowth and a great shaking of branches and leaves.

Valdez didn't wait around. He ran back along the stream, up and over the waterfall, around the eelbird pool, up the slippery slope, past the cave and back to the plateau. Breathing hard, he stopped beside the cooking pool and dropped the lobster and basket straight into the steaming water. It fizzed and bubbled and the basket jumped and twisted, then lay still.

How long does a lobster take to cook?

Valdez didn't know.

Better overcooked than undercooked.

He pulled up the basket often. When the lobster had changed from red to dark green, he decided it was done. He turned it out on to fresh, flat leaves and left it to cool. It looked like an ordinary lobster – about the length of his hand, with long, thin antennae, front claws as long as his thumb and a concertina tail. Its dark green top shell had one yellow stripe down the centre. Its four swimmer legs were yellow, too.

Valdez knew that the tail was the meatiest part. He flipped the lobster over with the knife and prodded the soft underside. It gave easily.

He couldn't wait any longer. Wrapping the lobster in a green leaf, he held the shell tight and sliced down the middle of the tail. The flesh fell open – pale, milky, a little underdone. Valdez scooped out a bit about the size of a small bean. It was still hot. He juggled it for a moment, then popped it into his mouth and held it there. He'd never had fresh lobster before, but it tasted just as he had expected – buttery and a little fishy. He bit down, mashed the flesh around and filled his mouth with juicy, sweet flavours. Trying to get all of the taste, he let the liquid dribble down the back of his throat and groaned with pleasure. It was good. No, better than good. It was the best food he'd ever had.

He scooped out the rest of the meat from the tail, then cracked open the shell. There wasn't a lot of meat there after he had flicked out some brown gooey waste. He broke off one of the claws, snapped it again at the joint and sucked the meat out of it. Same taste, but even sweeter. In a matter of minutes, he'd cleaned out all the meat, but the amount he had actually eaten was less than a handful. He didn't care. There were plenty more lobsters in the stream.

For the rest of the day, Valdez tripped back and forth to the rapids for more lobsters. He cooked and ate six of them, but took his time between meals. He didn't want to overpower his stomach with too much new food. On the last trip, he walked beyond the rapids and found another pool that fed into more fast-flowing water. There were plenty of red flashes there, too. Another good lobster spot.

As darkness fell across the forest and Valdez settled down for the night, he thought back over his time there. There had been many different types of days. There was crash day, cooking hole day, cave day, egg day, eelbird day and now lobster day. Lobster day had been the best day by far.

Patience and perseverance had given him a good supply of nourishing food. With the rest of the nuts and fronds, plus the berries and boiled vegetable, he could survive for a long time . . . as long as it took the rescuers to find him.

Again he felt pleased with himself. It wasn't a jump-up-and-down, scream-and-shout sort of pleasure. No. It was a warm, glowing, all-over feeling. A feeling he got from knowing he had achieved something really important.

CHAPTER SEVENTEEN

Sera was Valdez's sister in name only. He'd often wondered what had caused her to change. He knew of other famous people who, filled with their own importance, had become confused and lost all fairness and rationality. They became impossible to work with, and he could see how it might happen. Eco was to be the single most important development in the history of human civilisation. And Sera was mostly responsible for it. Now it was all threatened.

If Eco failed, Sera would lose everything – her job, her fame, her reputation. She would return to Earth humiliated and hated by the people whose hopes she had destroyed. Many times, Valdez had tried to talk to her about Umbro and how he could help, but it was impossible. She was always too busy. That was why their planned observation flight had been so important. If only she'd let Umbro help her. Why hadn't she? Valdez had no idea. His sister was a stranger.

Valdez woke suddenly. He was amazed how lightly he slept now. But what had woken him? He lay on his back listening. The night was still black. Dawn was a long way off. A puff of breeze blew over the cave ledge. He was sure he was alone and he couldn't hear any noises below. Apart from leaves rustling in the breeze, there were no noises at all. There should have been some animal coughing, squawking or barking. But there was nothing.

Silence had woken him.

The air had a tense, electric feel, as if something was about to happen. And then it started. A mighty roar. It was as if every living being in the forest had suddenly bellowed, slapped its body and clicked and snapped its limbs at the same time. He heard hollers, bleats, wails, cackles, chirps, croaks and hoots. Then came a mad rushing as branches snapped and leaf litter flew into the air.

Valdez stood at the cave entrance. He could just make out a sea of bustling, stomping bodies in the trees and along the forest floor.

A stampede.

But there was no direction to the rushing. It was as if the animals were terrified of something, but didn't know which way to escape. Then a rumble started far away. Valdez swayed on the ledge. Thinking he was losing his balance, he dropped to his knees. Suddenly, the ground lurched upwards then dropped with a deafening crack.

Earthquake.

The animals went into a frenzy, running ever faster, madly crashing into each other, smashing into trees. Valdez wasn't sure if he should stay where he was or move back into the cave.

Then another quake struck. This time the ground moved in great waves, rolling up and down. Then it suddenly stopped and shook so violently that Valdez was thrown backwards off his feet and crashed into a tall, sharp rock beside his bed. He grabbed hold of the rock to steady himself. Another quake hit and he wrapped his arms around the rock and held on.

He was flung up and down and side to side. The cave lifted and his bed slid across the floor, bounced up and flew over the ledge. He ducked as a huge piece of rock sheered off the cave roof, crashed to the floor and showered him with splinters. He heard great trees splitting their trunks and others crashing to the forest floor. There was gushing steam and exploding gas on the plateau. And still the quakes came, one after another, with just a few seconds between.

And then it was over, just as suddenly as it had begun. But a more frightening sound had started. Animals, hundreds of them, began to cry out in pain. Valdez covered his ears to block out the wailing. Slowly their cries died out as they crawled away to tend their wounds. Then everything was quiet again.

Valdez got to his feet. The tender skin on the inside of his forearms was torn and bleeding from holding on to the rock. He stared at it, then suddenly exploded. A great, boiling, stored-up rage was finally released. “Come on!” he shouted. “Is that all you’ve got? Is that all you can do?”

He shouted at the forest, the earth and the sky.

“You’re determined to break me! But it won’t happen! I’m strong! Stronger than I ever was. I’ve learned. Even a mighty earthquake won’t defeat me. I’ll survive. I will survive!”

And he truly believed it.

He sat in the cave for the rest of the night, talking to himself, going over his list of achievements and setbacks, and how each one had made him a tougher person – not more intelligent, just wiser and more comfortable with the person inside his skin. He knew there really was only one person he could rely on, and that was himself.

Throughout the night there were aftershocks – short, sharp jolts – that brought down more trees and loose rocks. Slowly, the shocks became fewer and further apart. By first light the earth had settled again and Valdez finally fell asleep on the hard floor.

He woke with sweat running off his head. The angle of the light told him it was well past midday. His mouth felt like leather. His body ached all over. Dried, crusted blood coated the inside of his arms. He was hungry and thirsty. He got to his feet and tried to stretch the aches out of his back and shoulders. The forest was quiet now – spookily quiet. He hurled a rock into the forest. Crashing through the trees, it sent roosting birds fluttering and shrieking to the treetops. Valdez nodded. It was good to know the earthquake had not destroyed everything.

He climbed slowly down the rock wall and rested at the bottom, shocked at the wreckage he saw around him. It was as if some giant monster had gone crazy, flinging its arms and legs about, demolishing everything in its reach. Great trees had been uprooted and tossed aside like twigs. Boulders from the rock wall above the cave had crashed downwards, splintering themselves and anything they landed on. Valdez shook his head, pleased that he'd had safe shelter in the cave.

The track to the plateau was blocked, but the way to the nut and frond trees was clear. After a few long gulps of fresh water from the cup trees, he set off for some food. The berries had really ripened in the last few days and were almost gone. So had the fronds. But there were still plenty of nuts, and lobster and vegetable to boil.

He ate and gathered as many nuts, fronds and berries as he could, then headed back to the cave. He was still amazed at the mess all around. It had changed the shape of the land completely. As well as the mass of broken vegetation, there were new mounds and hollows everywhere. The earthquake's epicentre must have been close.

Back at the cave, he put the day's food into a new rock safe then collected fresh bedding. There was plenty about. He found two long and two short branches for the frame then got armfuls of moss, green needles, soft leaves and spongy ferns and tossed them up and over the cave ledge. He'd make the bed later. Right now it was time to catch some lobster.

He grabbed the basket and set off down the slope, then suddenly stopped. The eelbird pool was empty. He walked slowly towards it, listening and watching. He couldn't see the eelbird, but that didn't mean it wasn't around. He saw where the earthquake had shifted the shape of the ground and opened up a large crack in the pool by the outflow. He guessed that the water and the eels had been sucked out there.

He stepped closer to the edge and saw three large, bluish, broken eggs on the bottom of the pool. Lying in the mud beside the shells were hundreds of tiny, stiff fingerlings. Even in the dim light, Valdez could see their shimmering purplepink skins.

Then he heard the eelbird. It gave out a long, lonely screech. The screeching came again and again, but it was moving away. There was no reason for it to stay. Its young were dead. Even though the eelbird had hurt him badly, he couldn't help feeling sorry for it. Sighing, he moved on around the pool and down to the rapids.

Night was falling. He worked quickly. He baited the basket, dropped it into the rapids, then hauled it out a few minutes later with a snapping lobster inside.

Hurrying to the plateau, he had to fight his way over, around and through the fallen foliage. It was dark when he arrived back, but he was still able to see that the earthquake had shaken everything up there, too. There were new upslopes, downslopes, fissures, cracks, steam vents, tiny geysers and mudpools. He hoped the cooking hole hadn't gone.

It hadn't.

It was still sending up wafts of steam from its simmering surface. Valdez dropped the basket in and the water bubbled and jumped around it. A few minutes later, he turned the lobster out on to some leaves and waited for it cool. Above him, the sky was cloudy but the moon was up. Every now and then, when a broken cloud scudded overhead, it lit up the plateau for a few moments. It was during one of these moments that a blue glint in the swamp caught Valdez's eye. He stood up and looked more closely. Whatever it was now looked more grey than blue. It was too big to be a tree stump. Then the moon moved back behind the clouds. When it reappeared, Valdez saw the nose of the shuttle. His mouth dropped open.

"The shuttle!" he shouted. "It's the shuttle."

The earthquake had brought it to the surface. He wanted to run to it. He didn't know why, except that it was his only connection with Home Base and Umbro. But he wouldn't be able to reach it easily in the swamp. Rushing to investigate could be dangerous.

He stared at the shuttle and thought about Umbro. Was he still inside? If he was, he wouldn't have survived as long as this.

The thought sent a shiver through his body. He wasn't sure he wanted to find out, but he knew he had to. The shuttle was at least forty paces away. And the swamp had many dangers – quicksand, hot spots, holes. And it was dark.

No.

Don't rush, he told himself. Be patient. Think everything through. Plan carefully.

So he cleared away the leftover lobster and walked back to the cave. Then he gathered up all the bedding, lumped it into one big pile, squashed it down and stretched out.

Valdez lay awake for a long time. His mind raced, trying to work out how he was going to get to the shuttle. He didn't think about what he might find inside. Even though he knew it wasn't possible, a small part of him wanted to go to the shuttle right then and there. But another part of him didn't want to go at all. That part of him was afraid of what he might find inside.

CHAPTER EIGHTEEN

Valdez opened his eyes. He felt refreshed. He was surprised he had slept so well. He wriggled on the bedding, squeezing the pinches and aches from his shoulders. The picture of the shuttle's nose was fixed in his mind. For the first time in a while, his stomach rumbled. It wasn't hunger, but nervous excitement – excitement that could easily bubble over if he didn't control it.

First things first, he told himself.

He got up, stretched properly, climbed down into the forest and drank from the cup trees. He collected what berries and fronds he could find, then filled his pockets with nuts. Questions kept popping into his mind.

Would he be able to reach the shuttle?

Had its emergency batteries run down?

Was it sending emergency signals?

Would a satellite pick up its form?

Was Sera still searching for him?

So many questions, but no answers.

Why wasn't he running through the forest, gathering all the bits and pieces he would need to reach the shuttle?

He knew the answer to that one.

Umbro.

Why hadn't he ejected? If he had, they would have met up by now. Umbro would have had a transmitter to send an emergency signal to Home Base. Umbro was his link with Home Base. Umbro had been the only person who knew the truth about the virus. Umbro could have saved Eco. But maybe he hadn't survived the crash.

The reappearance of the shuttle had made everything complicated again. Too much thinking, he told himself. Get moving. Get on. Catch some lobsters. He was feeling confused when he had to focus on survival.

He only wanted to make one fishing trip that day so, when he got to the rapids, he took off his coveralls. As he caught each lobster, he wrapped it in the fabric so it wouldn't escape. When he had six, he returned to the plateau and cooked them one after another. While they cooled, he went back to the edge of the swamp.

He tested the thick reeds with his weight. His boot sank slowly into the squelchy mud. Walking across the swamp was impossible, but the shuttle had flattened many trees and left their stumps exposed. His plan was to tie three long, thin tree trunks together. The trunks would be no thicker than the width of two arms and cleaned of all branches and leaves. After he'd lashed them together, he would lay them from the bank to the nearest stump, which was only ten paces away. Then he'd walk across the ramp to the stump, pull the ramp up and lay it across the swamp again to another stump.

Four moves should do it, he thought.

Yes.

A good plan.

The stampeding animals had made the ground close to the plateau rutted and messy, but the earthquake had thrown down many tree trunks. He easily found three the right length and width and set about stripping off the branches. After cleaning them up, he dragged them to the edge of the swamp, then cut an armful of reeds. He slit the reeds into four strips, then tied the strips together and lashed the ends of the trunks with them. He tied them tight, then rechecked the knots. Satisfied that they would hold, he stood the ramp on one end, balanced it there for a moment, then pushed it over. It fell straight, swishing through the reeds, and thumped onto a stump. Valdez grinned.

So far so good.

Now to test it. On his hands and knees, he crawled on to the narrow ramp. The trunks were young and full of sap and they sagged under his weight. Muddy water seeped between the gaps and soaked his legs, but the ramp held. Valdez crawled about halfway along, bounced up and down a bit to test its strength, then backed up. It was a good ramp.

Back on land, he quickly ate a couple of lobsters and a handful of boiled vegetable, then crawled back along the ramp to the stump. He found a firm place to stand among the stump's roots then dragged the ramp towards him, stood it up, balanced it and dropped it on to the next stump. It was exhausting work. His back hurt and his arms ached, but slowly he closed the gap to the shuttle.

Almost two hours later and five shifts of the ramp, he finally crawled onto the front edge of the shuttle's wing. He lay there, breathing hard, not moving, trying to get some strength back into his body.

He rolled over and saw the forward pod above him. He pulled himself up and stared through the dark-tinted lid. He couldn't see anything. He ran his hands over the fuselage, searching for a hole or loose join – something that would let him in. At last he found a slit in the nose, down low, close to where the wing joined the body.

He opened the knife, dug the blade into the expandable, mesh-metal skin and dragged it through the soft material. He got his hand under an edge and pulled upward then dug the knife deeper. Caught on something, it twisted in his hand and spun away, landing point-first on the ramp. There it quivered for a moment, stuck in the wood.

Valdez glanced at it, then turned back to the slit. He didn't need the knife. Grabbing handfuls of the shuttle's outer skin, he tugged and ripped a bigger hole. He reached in, felt around and touched Umbro's smooth boot.

"Aaargh!" he yelled.

Valdez slid down the wing and slumped on to the ramp. His stomach heaved. He spat and coughed up chunks of lobster and vegetable.

"Stop," he said, shaking his head to clear it. "Stop thinking scared. Umbro's dead. He's been dead for days. Nothing's changed."

He had to go back in. If there was anything useful there, he had to find it. He pushed himself to his knees and shook his head again. A nagging buzz, like the one the hair-pullers made, was in his ears. Now the buzz changed to heavy fluttering. Soon it was directly above him, a thundering blast, sending twigs, leaves, branches and stones whirling into the air.

A shuttle! It hovered over the plateau, then dropped quickly and landed on the rocks.

Valdez didn't move. He stood on the ramp unable to believe his ears and eyes. One moment he was all alone, about to search a pod that held a dead man, and the next moment there was a shuttle on the plateau.

He nodded his head slowly, gradually understanding that his rescuers had come. His time on the bare, inhospitable, isolated plateau was over. He slumped to knees, his hands shaking violently. He reached out and pulled the broken knife out of the tree trunk to stop the shaking, but the quivering started all over again when he saw Sera.

She hurried to the edge of the swamp, waving and calling his name.

"We've searched all over for you. All the shuttle's emergency transmitters are dead. Satellites only picked up the shuttle's shape this morning. We came straight away."

Valdez stood up. He didn't know what to say or what to do. When he opened his mouth and tried to speak, all that came out was a dry rasp. He coughed, touched the side of the shuttle and tried again.

"Umbro's here. He's inside. He's dead."

CHAPTER NINETEEN

Valdez stared across the swamp at his sister. She was grinning. How could she be so happy after all she had done? Where was her conscience?

"Umbro's dead!" he shouted. "And it's all your fault!"

Sera's smile turned to a frown. Then she turned and went over to her shuttle. She came back with tools, bundles of mesh rope, mesh matting, long, thin poles and two crew members. They laid the gear out and set about joining all the bits together to make a long, narrow, lightweight, fine-meshed mat, which they rolled out from the edge of the swamp. Small puddles of swamp water seeped through the mesh as they walked over it towards him, but it supported all three of them easily.

When they got within a few paces of Valdez, he suddenly shouted, "Stop there!"

Sera frowned. "What's wrong?"

"Don't make out that you don't know. It's you. You're a traitor. You allowed the virus to spread unchecked. You're probably the one who caused it. You've destroyed Eco!"

Sera glanced at the other crew then spoke quietly. "I'm not the traitor. It was Umbro. He spread the virus."

Valdez shook his head. "That's easy to say, now that he's dead. I heard you in the lab. I heard you with Umbro. I heard Umbro, again and again, say how you were so stubborn, unreasonable and narrow-minded. If you weren't so proud, so superior . . . If you'd let him help you, he could've . . . together, you could've saved Eco. And the immigrants would have been able to land."

"You're wrong," said Sera, "and I'll prove it."

She raised her hands a little then said, "We're coming on to the shuttle. I need to get inside. I need to get to Umbro to show you."

The crew moved closer to Sera then followed her on to the shuttle's wing. Valdez moved up behind the pod, out of their way.

Using hand-cutters and hand-grips they ripped the hole in the pod wider. Then Sera crawled in through the hole. Valdez heard snapping and clicking, then Umbro's helmet rolled out of the hole. Sera backed out slowly and held Umbro up, or what was left of him.

He hung limp in his coveralls, as if every bone in his body was broken. His head, a shaggy, hollow mask, looked ghostly. His body sagged and twisted unnaturally. Sera flipped him over. A long zipper split his back open, showing a plastic and metal skeleton beneath.

Valdez gasped and slid down on to the wing. He grabbed the human suit, squeezed the fake flesh, stared at the empty eyes and felt the lifelike hair.

"What's this? What's going on?"

Sera passed the deflated body to one of the crew, then took Valdez by the elbow and led him back over the mesh mat to the plateau.

"Umbro wasn't one of us," she said. "One of the reasons we've had so many problems on Eco is because of him. He's sabotaged us every chance he got – poisoning water supplies, altering animal genetics, changing balances in habitats . . . and introducing the virus."

Valdez shook his head in confusion. "In the lab

I heard Umbro say you didn't care. He said the damage was done and that he'd never get the . . . the antidote."

Sera nodded. "I had found out that he was the saboteur. I told him that I had reported him to the Federation of Planets and that they were sending guards to arrest him."

She pointed at the two crewmen. They had Umbro's body shape stretched out on the rocks and were moving scanners inside and outside the synthetic skin.

"Umbro is . . . he's still alive somewhere. He's an android and an impostor. He's also a scientist, but his Federation qualifications and experience were false. When the virus struck, all Eco inhabitants were security screened. But Umbro wasn't in the system."

Valdez was beginning to understand. "You said he's still alive."

One of the crew, a small, heavy-browed man, joined them. "Umbro is able to rearrange his cell structures to imitate any being of similar size or mass," he said. "His state of change can be instant or it can be delayed for as long as he wants."

Valdez remembered the blinding light in the

shuttle pod. "So he could be floating around us at this very moment, watching and listening?"

The man smiled and shook his head. "When he exited the shuttle after deactivating all emergency systems, he left the planet. He's up there somewhere now, speeding towards another world on which to cause havoc. Why does he do this? The Federation's not absolutely sure, but we think he's a disturbed, displaced alien. Every time he lands on a new planet, he hopes it's his long-lost home. And, when he discovers it's not, he gets angry and tries to destroy it."

Sera nodded. "He's like the virus – unknown make-up, uncontrollable and capable of causing huge devastation."

Suddenly, Valdez saw how everything fitted together. His knees sagged. He felt weak. I was wrong about Sera, he thought. I was wrong about Umbro. Sera is good and Umbro is evil. Umbro's monstrous mutterings about Sera were all part of his performance – his performance to get me to believe that Sera was bad. And it worked. Umbro – it's so hard to believe – betrayed us. I worked with him, talked with him, laughed with him. I thought he was my friend, not my enemy.

Valdez shook his head. Umbro had been so convincing. And his vicious work still wasn't finished.

"But what about the virus?" Valdez asked.

Sera frowned. "Well, that's another problem. We created a successful antidote, but Umbro wiped all record of it from the database. The trials were complete and we'd made one batch, but then we couldn't duplicate it – Umbro again. Luckily, I had the first batch. I kept it with me always. I had it with me when we were on our way to the shuttle to take that flight with you."

"So you didn't pull out of the flight?"

Sera shook her head. "I got a call to go to the hangar to pick up some new sample collectors. It was a hoax. Umbro was waiting for me. He had escaped from his guards."

She shrugged and sighed. "We fought, but he easily overpowered me and stole the antidote. Then he boarded the shuttle with the two most important things in my life – you and the antidote vial. He wanted to destroy both."

She touched Valdez's arm. "You cannot be replaced, but we can replace the antidote . . . eventually. By the time we've done it, though,

Eco's oxygen atmosphere will be too depleted for people to live outdoors. The immigrants have been ordered back to Earth. More immigrants will come, but not for a while. It will take half a lifetime for the rainforest, grasslands and tundra habitats to produce enough oxygen to rebalance Eco's atmosphere."

Valdez had only heard half of what she'd said. He was searching his pockets. "If you had the antidote now, would that make a difference?" he asked her.

Sera frowned. "Of course. It would make all the difference. We could manufacture huge quantities. We'd seed rain clouds with antidote vapour then create great storms over the affected areas. The antidote rains would wipe out the virus in a few short weeks and the immigrants . . . "

She stopped. Her eyes grew wide. Valdez had the knife and was pointing to the small vial fixed into the handle. Sera grabbed it and tried to pry it free. It wouldn't budge. She gave it to the crewman and he pulled the knife blade right back on to the handle. The vial popped free.

Sera held the vial up to the light and grinned.

For a moment they stared awkwardly at each

other, then Sera grabbed Valdez and hugged him so tight he gasped. He hugged her back just as hard. At last he knew everything was going to be all right.

When they eventually separated, Valdez walked over to the cooking hole and picked up the leftover lobster. He grinned as he held it up for Sera and her crew to see. "Is anyone hungry?" he asked.